YANCEY

GARY MCMILLAN

Cover Concepts and Design By
Michael McMillan

Authors' Discovery Cooperation
11308 West Kassnar Dr.
Odessa, Texas 79764
432-381-4318

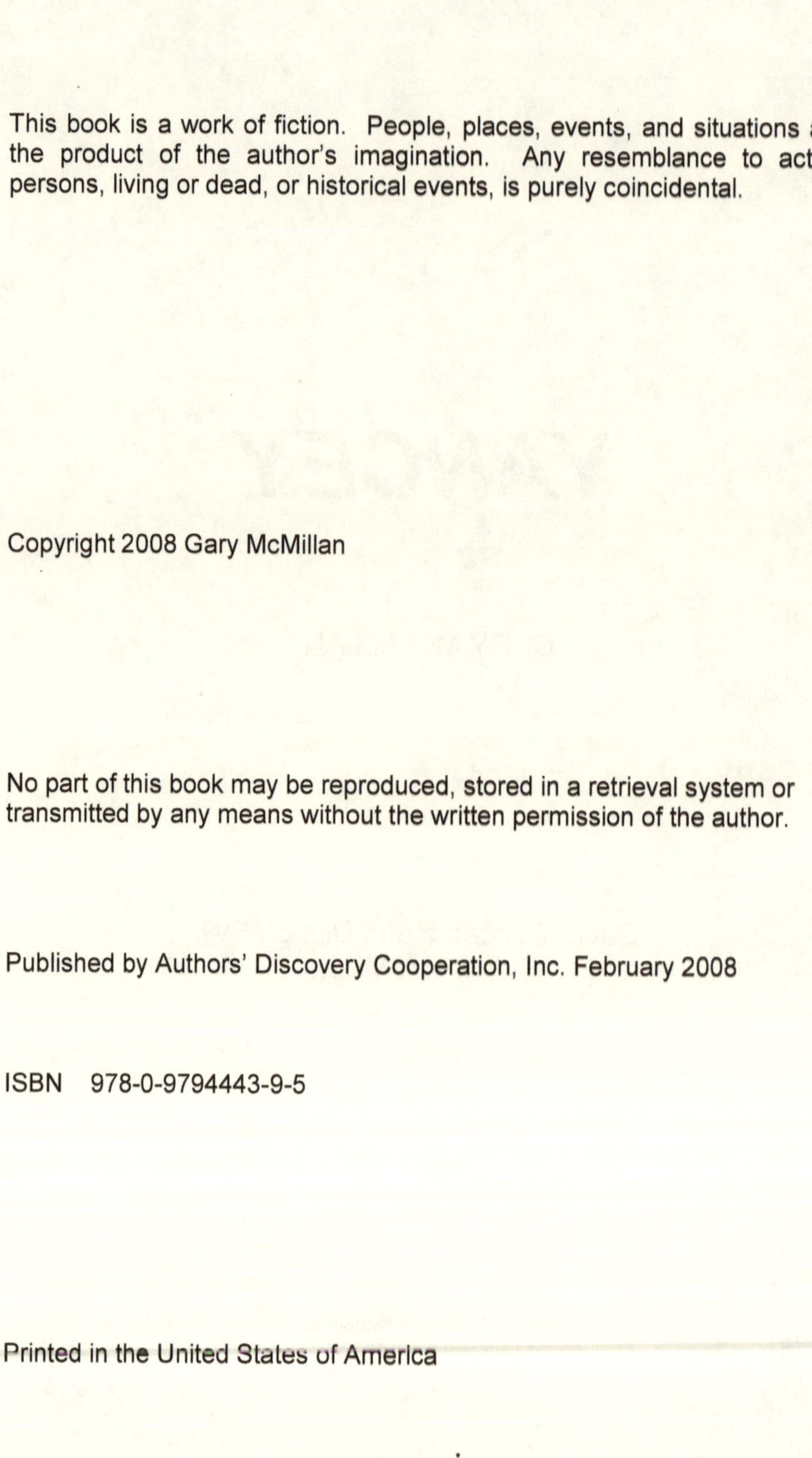

This book is a work of fiction. People, places, events, and situations are the product of the author's imagination. Any resemblance to actual persons, living or dead, or historical events, is purely coincidental.

Copyright 2008 Gary McMillan

No part of this book may be reproduced, stored in a retrieval system or transmitted by any means without the written permission of the author.

Published by Authors' Discovery Cooperation, Inc. February 2008

ISBN 978-0-9794443-9-5

Printed in the United States of America

ABOUT THE AUTHOR

Gary was born and raised in Texas. He loves reading stories of the men and women who risked all to settle the "Old West". As a boy growing up, his parents only allowed three types of reading material in their home, the Bible, western books and western magazines.

Gary found the history of Fort Clark Springs very interesting. He spent the last twenty-five years visiting Fort Clark and researching the history of this particular Fort. He decided to write a series of books about the problems along the Texas-Mexico Border shortly after the Civil war. This is the third book in the series.

OTHER BOOKS IN THE TYE WATKINS SERIES

BORDER TROUBLE
THE CROSSING

PREFACE

Tye's father, Ben Watkins, had been a well know mountain man in the 'shinning times' of the beaver craze from the early 1800's to about 1836. When the days of the mountain man ended, Ben decided to go to the new State of Texas where there was plenty of room. He met Lori in San Antonio, married, and built a home close to the Rio Grande. It was a rough and dangerous land along the Texas, Mexico Border in 1839 when Tye was born. When Tye was old enough to walk, Ben began teaching him all the skills he would need to survive this country: tracking, hunting, fighting, and shooting. Over the years, Tye honed these skills until he became the best scout in Texas, feared by the bandits and respected by the Apaches.

Shakespeare McDovitt was one of the few remaining original mountain men. He had trapped with Jim Bridger and his best friend, Ben Watkins during the beaver craze of the twenty's and thirty's in the Rockies and the Yellowstone. He had heard that his old friend had been killed down in Texas by the Apaches. Shakespeare was now seventy-one years old and had made his way to Fort Clark to meet his old friend's son, Tye.

Tye was Chief of Scouts at Fort Clark. Shakespeare wanted to tell Tye things about his father that he knew Ben probably never told him. His stories were interrupted by the usual problem in this part of the country, Apache trouble and border bandits.

Chapter One

Shakespeare was finding sleep hard to come by this night. He was more than just a little uptight about the event that would take place in the morning. A great number of mountain men were still living, but not many of the original trappers were still above ground... He had trapped beaver with Jim Bridger and Ben Watkins for years back in the twenties and early thirties before the high demand for beaver fur dropped off back east, marking an end to the mountain man. Ben Watkins was his best friend back then and he was the reason Shakespeare was now in Fort Clark, Texas. Ben had been killed a few years earlier but had written a letter to Shakespeare years before, inviting him to come live with him, his wife, and young son. Shakespeare had carried the letter for over twenty years and several times had started down to see Ben but something always came up that prevented his going. Ben was gone now and Shakespeare intended to meet his son, Tye, before he checked it in himself. He was seventy-one years old and knew time was running out. Upon arriving at Clark, he learned Tye, who was Chief of Scouts, was on patrol but was due back any time. Major Thurston, Post Commander at Clark, let Shakespeare stay in Tye's old quarters that wasn't being used since Tye was now married.

"Ta hell with trin' ta sleep," he mumbled to himself as he got out of bed. He stumbled into the kitchen and found the lamp and after lighting it, started looking for the coffee pot and coffee. When the water was boiling, he dropped in the grounds and the aroma immediately filled the room. Pouring himself a cup, he sat down at the table fixing to take his first swallow when he was surprised by someone knocking on the door.

"Whu's thar?

"Corporal Henning. Major Thurston wants you to come to the hospital."

"Huspital? Whut fur

"The patrol came in and Tye has been wounded."

"Hold on thar sunny, I'll be rite thar." He pulled his moccassin boots on and opened the door. "Leed tha way."

Arriving at the hospital, Shakespeare immediately saw Thurston and the 'purtiest' dang woman he ever did see. Thurston came over to him and shook his hand while introducing him to the girl.

"Shakespeare, this lady is Rebecca Watkins, Tye's wife, and Rebecca, this man is Shakespeare McDovitt." Rebecca had a startled look on her face as she reached to shake the man's hand.

"Ben's friend?"

"Yes'um, I wus Ben's fren bac in them days. Been a long time ago."

Rebecca hugged him tightly, tears running down her cheeks. "Shakespeare, you don't know how happy this will make, Tye," she cried. "He's told me a hundred times he wished he could talk to someone from back then that knew his father."

"Tye's coming," Thurston said. Tye appeared shirtless, his arm in a sling. Rebecca pulled away from Shakespeare and ran to him, throwing her arms around his neck, kissing him.

"Let's go home," Tye said after he acknowledged the major and shaking his hand.

"There's someone you need to meet, Tye," Rebecca said as she led Tye by the hand to where Shakespeare was standing. Shakespeare was staring at a ghost. Tye was the spitting image of his father, tall, blue eyed, muscular, and good looking.

"Tye, this is Shakespeare McDovitt," she said, as the two men shook hands.

"Little battle tested thar ain't ya?" Shakespeare said, noticing the scars on Tye's bare torso.

"Glad to meet you old timer," Tye said. He took Rebecca's hand. "Let's go, honey." He turned and took a couple steps.

"Sum peeple call me Buff," Shakespeare said. Tye stopped in mid-stride and looking back at the little man, asked.

"What did you say?"

"Sum ole boy bac in twentee-six by tha name uf Ben gave me that thar name." Tye looked at Rebecca.

She nodded her head. "It's Shakespeare honey, your pa's friend from the mountains." Tye stood motionless, staring at Shakespeare.

"That true?"

"I wus yur pa's fren bac then, Tye. Kame all tha way heer to see ya while I still kud." Tye took two full strides up to the man and pulled him to his chest with his good arm.

"Shakespeare...here...my God," he said, his voice cracking.. Rebecca was crying again and even Shakespeare was tearing up. Thurston handed Rebecca his handkerchief, excusing himself from the emotional scene. Tye, pulling back and getting control of his emotions, took Rebecca's hand. "Let's all go home honey. We all have a lot to talk about," he said, looking at Shakespeare

"I got me a lot uf storees ta tell ya abut yur pa, Tye."

"Pa told me a thousand stories of you, him and Bridger and those years trapping beaver in the Rockies and the Yellowstone."

"I kno Ben problee told ya a lot uf them but Ben wern't no braggin' man so I'm shor he didn't tel ya everee thang he did. He wus a man ta ride tha river with, Tye, and I wus proud ta kall him my fren."

"Buff, I have wanted for years, prayed for years, to find out more about pa and now you're here...why? How come after all this time?

"Ben wus tha best fren I ev'r had. Tore my hart out when I heerd he had got himself kilt. I been wuntun ta cum down heer fur yeers, ev'r sence I got tha letter frum Ben but sumthang always cum up. I'm gettin sorta long in tha tooth and I wunted ta see Ben's son afore I checked it in. I cum ta see ya, Tye."

"Shakespeare McDovitt," Tye said putting his good arm around the little man. "Yes, sir, we've got a lot of talking to do." The three of them headed toward Los Moras Creek and Tye's and Rebecca's home.

~~~

At the house, Tye and Shakespeare sat at the table while Rebecca was pouring the coffee. She sat down with them and there was an awkward moment of silence before Shakespeare spoke up.

"Been waiting all this heer time ta talk ta ya and now, I don't kno whar ta start."

"How about when you first met my pa?"

"Tha musta been abut tweeny-five or tweeny-six at tha rondavue we monton men had ever yeer. Thar's always a lot uf games like hors racin, rasling, shootin, and knock'um down bar knukel fiting as wale as sellin and tradin the beever plews. This yeer, thar wus this big, strappin kid abut tweeny yeers old tha wus winnin ever rasling match and bare knukle fite with tha older men. This heer wun man wus sorta embarssed by lusing ta this heer yung pup so he got hisself two uther men ta help him and they jumped this yungun. Jim Bridger and me saw it. It wus a hell uf a fite and this yung whippersnapper wus holdin his own agan tha three uf them. We went in and Bridger kold kocked wun with his rifle butt and I did anuther wun. Tha uther wun ran off and this heer yungster was
~~~

madder hell at us fur spoilin his fun. Jim liked him rite off and gav him a invite ta join our trappin partee even tho' he was a greener than anee wun I ev'r saw. Didn't kno wun end of a beever frum the uther but ole Jim liked him an tha wus it. Tha wus how I met yur pa, Tye. He wus a fast lerner an weren't no problum ta kno one. We becum inseprable frens pretee quik like and as tha say...tha rest is histree."

Tye set down his cup. "Pa use to say...he was interrupted by a knock on the door. Rebecca got up to see who it was.

"Tye, its Lieutenant Garrison and the O'Malley's," she said, opening the door for them to come in.

"Tye, if it's not a problem, we would like to meet Shakespeare?" Sergeant O'Malley said. O'Malley was Rebecca's dad's brother. When her father and mother were killed up north by the Comanche, she had come to live with the O'Malley's. First Sergeant O'Malley was a career soldier. He had joined the army in '57 and distinguished himself during the War. He came to Fort Clark when the fort was regarrisoned in '66. He was big and he was tough, just as a recruit would expect from his sergeant. He was tough but he was fair and the men loved him. They knew under that rough demeanor was a teddy bear and had feelings for his men. They loved him. He had introduced Rebecca to Tye several months ago and was elated when they had married. He knew Tye was tough as nails and meaner than a she bear with cubs, but he was a man, one whose word was his bond and would die before breaking it.

"Get over here and grab a chair," Tye said. After all the introductions were made and more coffee put on the stove Tye spoke up. "All of you have heard me speak of pa and his years in the mountains trapping beaver. You also heard me speak of his friend, 'Buff'. Well, Shakespeare is Buff. That's a nick name my pa gave him and what he was called by everyone."

"Ben wus a fun luvin man and wus great at givin names to ever wun." Shakespeare said. "I was 'Buff' which wus short fur buffalo. He gave it ta me after I damn neer got myself kilt by a buff I had shot an tho't he wus dead. Damn neer kilt me when I stuck my skinn' nife in him." he said chuckling. "I guess tha funn'st wun tho wus tha wun he gave Jerome Absher. Absher was six three if'n he wus a inch but onlee wayed abut one hundert and fiftee pounds. Skinner than a fence post he wus. Ben gave him tha name, Stumpee. Name stuck with him tha wrest uf his life."

"Go ahead Buff. Keep talking, we're all ears," O'Malley said.

Buff leaned back in his chair and shut his eyes. "That ferst yeer wus a grate yeer fur beever. Like I sad a minite ago, yung Ben kaught on quik and wus naver a probleem fur enee wun. Twer't much injun probleems as uf yet. At tha rondavou that yeer, we all made a gud profeet on our plews. Tha second yeer wus evn bettar. Ben had becum a ferst class trapp'r and me an him had becum gud frens. Thar wus sumthang else in tha air this spring as we heedad ta our rondavuee: injun truble."

"Truble wus cumin an ever wun in our partee knu it. We rode in single file, rifles out uf theer fur sheaths, redee fur it when it kame. Thar wur 'leven of us in all, sum uf us Americuns an sum wur Frenchmen. Jim Briger wus tha 'booshway' of tha partee but a Frenchman by tha name uf Lafeet, whu wus familur with tha trale, wus leeding us. We wur haded fur our annul monton man randevuee in tha Green Rivur Cuntree. Eech man's pak horse wus loded down with prime beever plews fur sale an trade thar. It wus fortee mile as tha crow flies but problee close tu a hundert by tha trale we had ta take." He was interupted by Garrison.

"What's a booshway?"

"Tha leeder uf tha partee. Lootenant uf tha patrol so ta speek." Buff replied.

"Well, what's a beaver plew?"

"Beever pelt, sunny. How long ya been out heer frum bac east?"

"Bout four months."

"That thar abut whut I figgered. Yu don't kno nuttin abut nuttin. Damn greener ya are."

"What's a greener?" Lieutenant Garrison asked.

"Greenhorn. Wun tha kno's nuttin abut nuttin." Buff said smiling as everyone else was laughing. Garrison joined in, laughing with everyone else.

Shakespeare was right about Garrison being a little green as far knowing about things. He didn't know that for the short time Garrison had been at Clark, his first assignment after graduating from the Point, he had become a damn good officer. He had been on patrol with Tye when they brought in Alex Vasquez back in July. He was wounded in the fight with Alex's gang. Garrison wanted to make the army a career and had requested to be assigned to a frontier outpost. He didn't know country like the arid region around Clark even existed having been raised back east. He had come to love this area around Clark, no longer looking at it as a desert like his first impression was. Like the post commander, Major Thurston, he wanted to make this country a safer place for a man to raise a family. Tye thought highly of him as an officer and they had become good friends.

"This heer storee tellin may take a while if'n I keep gettin' qustions frum this heer greener." Everyone laughed again. When things settled down, Buff took up the story.

"Like I sade befor, we all knu truble wus cummin. Tha Blackfut had always been frendly with us trapp'rs but I guess tha had enuff of mor'n and mor'n uf us cummin into theer land and killin off tha game tha needed. Thar had been reports of trapp'rs bein kilt by them, so we wur reddy."

"Me, Bridger, Stumpee and all tha rest wur seasoned trappers...all exceptin yung Ben. We all been in fites befo with injuns exceptin him. We wus ridin across a flat mesa when I heerd tha 'thunk', an Lafeet wus fallin off his horse, an arror tip stickin frum his back. Thar wus no panik amung tha trappers as Bridger tuk control and led a retreet bac tha way we had cum. We quicklee saw that wus no gud...thirtee or more Blackfoot blocked tha trale. Thar were fiftee or more cuming frum tha other way and now we were in a pikle. Luking around, Bridger spotted a large deadfall and led tha men toward it. Arriving, we wur suprised to fin a depreshion large enugh fur all of us ta get into. Bridger had two men piket tha horses at tha veree bac uf tha depreshion, maybee thirtee feet away frum whare we lay."

"Thar wus still no panik amung tha partee. We felt we wur in a gud spot, below ground level and a large deadfall all around. Tha Blackfut wus taking their time, knowing we were not going anywhere. The two groups were together now and looked to be close to a hundred warriors. When they came, it was with screems frum every one uf them. A screeming charge like this made even tha most seesoned uf us trappr's hair stand up on tha back of his nek an his blud run kold. We waited, picking our targets, and at fortee yards, cut loose with our long rifles and followed with our single shot pistols. We were all excellent shots and there wasn't many misses and the affect was devastating to tha Blackfut war party. Thar wus a lot uf hooting and hollering when tha 'Red Devils' turn-tailed and ran bac to tha trees. Musta been abut eighteen or twenty horses tha had no riders. All tha arrors lusened at us during tha attack wure in tha dirt walls or sticking in tha fallen logs...not a single injury amung us," he said.

Buff took another sip of coffee before continuing..."Bridger shut every wuh up, sade it wasn't over an I tale yu now, no truer words wur ever spoken. It wus not over, but continued in a way none uf us ever emagined. Tha sun wus almost bloked out by tha arrors that filled tha sky. The arrors seemed to be in slow motion as tha silently sliced upward, thru tha air, befo starting their downward plunge. Lying in tha depression, we huddled close together, wishing we could disappear. Looking up, we watched, waited fur death ta rain on us."

Shakespeare paused for a second, shaking his head and breaking out in a cold sweat just remembering. That had been the scariest moment in all of his years trapping beaver. "Tha damn Blackfut, hiding bac in tha trees, wur shuting their arrors toward tha sky and letting them fall among us." Shakespeare paused... he could still hear the screams of the men as wave after wave of arrows plowed into their bodies. "I can still smell tha dirt as I tried ta bury myself under it. I kan still smell tha blud of my dying friends. Onliest time I kan member being skeered my whol life.Thar wur only four uf us left uf tha partee, Bridger, Watkins, Stumpee, an myself. Stumpee had an arror thru his leg but tha four uf us lived becauz we used tha bodies of our ded frens to kuver us. Our frens luked like pin kushions. Tha four uf us eskaped later only becauze anuther large partee uf trappers showed up, and twix them and us, drove tha Blackfut warrors away. Fur fortee yeers now, I have kept that storee to my own self, not tellin no wun. Always wundered abut usin my frens tha way...wundered if'n God abuv wuld be upset with me."

There was complete silence in the room. Everyone's thoughts were what it must have been like to go through something like that. Rebecca finally broke the silence.

"I can assure you that no one, including God, would condemn you for what each of you did. That must have been a horrible experience for each of you. I can't even imagine..." she was cut off by Tye.

"Certainly, no one could blame you, Shakespeare. I, as probably each man here, would have done the same thing. A man will do a lot of things when he's in a life or death situation and there is no time to think."

Shakespeare nodded his head. "Glad yu all feel tha way. Feel bettur fur getting it off my chest aftur all theese yeers."

"How about something to drink, honey?" Tye said to Rebecca. “I know it's a little early but this is a special day. How about it Shakespeare; thirsty for a shot?"

"Ain't ev'r been knowed ta turn down a drink," Shakespeare answered. Rebecca poured the men a drink and replenished her's and Mrs. O'Malley's coffee cup. Shakespeare stood up and said, "Here's ta Tye an ta tha memoree of my best fren, Ben," as he held up his cup in a toast. Everyone else did likewise, and then downed their drinks.

"Wun other thang befor we go anee further, Tye. I got sumthang fur yu. Be bac in a minute." He got up and walked to his saddle bags that was in the spare room and took a letter out.

"Onliest lettur I ev'r got in my whol life an it's frum yur pa, Tye. It's my most prized posession. Nev'r lerned ta reed or rite but frens red it ta me manee times ov'r tha yeers. It's yur’s now, Tye," he said, handing it to Tye.

Tye reached out with a trembling hand and gingerly took the worn, yellowed envelope from Shakespeare. He stared at it for a minute in disbelief... a letter written by pa over twenty years ago. He turned it so he could read the front. He could make out a few of the letters but not whole words. Too many years and the weather had taken its toll.

"Open it up, honey," Rebecca whispered. Tye looked at everyone then slowly and carefully opened the envelope. He took the worn and yellowed letter out and laid it very carefully on the table, spreading it out flat with his hands. He stared at it for a moment, saying nothing. Looking at a letter, written by his pa when Tye was only a small child, was a very special moment. His eyes quickly scanned the letter and settled on a crude map at the bottom. He recognized the area, the landmarks, and the 'x' marking his parents old homestead.

"What does it say, Tye?" Rebecca asked. Tye swallowed, trying to clear the lump from his throat.

"It's addressed to Shakespeare and dated April 6, 1844." He began to read the letter struggling over each faded word.

Shakespeare old friend,

I hope this letter finds you in good health. I sent it to the last address I had. Figured you will get it eventually...everyone knows you. I have settled in Texas and it sure isn't the mountains but I love it. It's wide open country and lots of free land for the taking. I married a beautiful woman by the name of Lori whom I met in San Antonio. She's a wonderful lady and and loves this country as I do. I know you like elbow room so you may like to know our nearest nabor is about seventeen miles away. We have a son now. Named him Tye. He's five now and he is going to be something special. He takes to tracking and hunting like bees go for honey. Going to be a big kid too. He's already a good shot and had rather sleep under the stars than in a bed. I never knew the wonderful feeling a man could have by having a wife and child that he adores and cherishes more'n anything in the world.

Shakespeare, I want you to think of something...seriously. We have a large house with a extra room. I know you have no folks and if you have not got yourself hitched and still roaming around the country, we would like you to come live with us...as family. I have drawn a map at the bottom of the page. An old tracker like yourself should have no problem finding us.

I'm serious about your coming old friend. We'd sincerely love to have you join our family. Hope to see you soon. Take care, old friend.

Your friend Ben

Tye sood up, excused himself, and walked thru the door out on the porch. Shakespeare started to get up but Rebecca put her hand on his shoulder.

"Let him be for a moment, Buff. All this is pretty emotional for him." Buff sat back down understanding what she meant as did everyone else.

Lieutenant Garrison, looking over his shoulder at Tye on the porch, turned back around and asked, "We missed the part of how you met Ben, can you tell us a little more about him?"

"Tha mane thang ya need ta kno sunny wus this. I met him at tha rondovu in '26. He joined our partee because Bridger invited him. He wus green but lerned fast. I trapped with all uf the best trappr's, Bridger, Coulter, Johnson, Fitzpatric, Walker, yu name'un, I knu'um. Ben ended up tha best uf tha bunch, at leest in my opinun. Brav'st man I ev'r knu...wusn't frade uf ole lucifur himself and hell on wheels in a fite."

"What, after all these years, made you decide to come all the way down to Texas?" Sergant O'Malley asked. Shakespeare took a drink before answering.

"Best frend I ev'r had wus Ben." He sat back in his chair, smiled, and with a chuckle said, "We had us sum grate times...yes sir, sum grate times. Those wur tha gud ole days with tha onliest thang wun had ta wurry abut wus trying ta keep frum freezing ta death in winter, keeping yur scalp frum being on a Blackfut's lance, and finden beever. Afta tha demand fur beever stopped, we sorta went our own ways, Ben, Jim, Stumpy, and me. We sade we wud sta in tuch with eech uther. Didn't happ'n tho. Ben wus tha onliest wun that did." He picked up the letter, looked at it for a second, and laid it carefully back down on the table. "After I got tha letter frum Ben, I told myself tha I wus going ta see my old fren. Kan't tell ya how many times I started, but sumthang always cum up and I culdn't go."

He looked away, staring out the open window. "Hurd a few yeers ago that Ben got himself kilt by sum 'Paches. Biggest regret of my life wus not cuming ta see him in time. Then, I started heering stories bout this yung scout that wus making quite a name fur himself down in Texas...scout by tha name uf Watkins. Herd tell his pa had been a mounton man. I figgered it wus Ben's son so I decided I wun't gonna make tha same mistake twice. I wuz gonna meet him afore I cheked it in myself, and heer I am."

"I'm glad you did," Rebecca said reaching over the table and patting Shakespeare on the shoulder. Tye came back in and sat down.

"My pa invited you to stay with us all those years ago." He looked up at Rebecca and she knew what was coming, and she nodded her head giving him the go ahead. "You never got married did you?"

"Nope. No desent woman ev'r wunted a old geezer like me," he said laughing. Rebecca stood up and walked around the table and kissed him on the cheek. "I find that hard to believe, Buff." Buff reached up and touched the spot on his cheek, embarrased.

"Well, your traveling days are over my friend. We want you to live here...with us...as family. We have a spare room and we won't take no for an answer." Shocked at the offer, Shakespeare was finding words hard to come by.

"I...well...I don't...don't kno whut ta say," he finally stammered out. "I don't wunt ta be no burden. Always pade my own way. Don't have no job down hear."

"Listen, Shakespeare" Tye butted in. "The last few years I have run down a lot of bandits and Apaches. We live on the fort but people are coming and going all the time.

When I'm on scout, I worry one of the friends of some of them would sneak in here and harm Rebecca. If you were here, I would not have that worry."

"Are ya serous abut that, Tye? Wuld it help? Yur not jus saying that?"

"Hell no...I'm serious. You've been on scout and you know how important it is to keep your mind on what you're doing...not let your mind wander to other problems or worries. It could get you killed." Shakespeare nodded in agreement.

"Nev'r had no wun ta wurry abut but I see whut ya meen. Sounds gud, Tye, but let's wait a few days and see if'n thangs work out. I ain't ever had me no real home ya kno."

"Okay, Buff." Tye replied. "We'll give it a few days but the decision will be yours, because Rebecca and me are sure."

"Nothing could change our minds, Buff. You will be family," Rebecca said coming around the table and hugging Buff's neck again. Buff stood up and excused himself saying he needed a breath of fresh air, walked to the door and stepped outside. He sat down on the steps to think and regain his composure. Seventy-one years old and now, at this late stage of his life, had a chance to live in a home with people he cared about...and cared about him. He could not remember ever shedding a tear over anything and now, he had twice in a couple hours. Here he was at this late stage of his life and for the first time he could remember, a real home…a home with a roof, walls, a fireplace to keep him warm in the winter, and people he cared for who seemed to care for him. All his life the mountains had been his walls, the sky his roof, and the pine trees and the beautiful aspens his décor. He had no relatives and most of his old friends were dead. "If I had died yesterday, no one would have missed me. Now…it's…it's different," he whispered.

Tye waited a few minutes knowing full well why Buff went outside. He and Rebecca had given understanding looks at each other with Rebecca placing her finger to her lips, signaling him to be quite. Tye waited a little longer then stood up, walked outside and placed his arm around Buff's shoulders. "Gotta go see the major with Garrison and O'Malley; you want to go with us?" Buff nodded, keeping his back toward the men. Together, they walked to Thurston's office.

Chapter Two

"What's up Major?" Tye asked as they entered Thurston's office. He had to wait for an answer as the army formalities of saluting was being taken care of between Thurston, Garrison, O'Malley, and the major shaking Buff's hand.

"Don't know for sure, Tye...maybe nothing. There's been a report of drums beating pretty steady for three days now plus sightings of an unusual number of Apaches."

"Where?" Tye asked. Thurston walked to the wall map and placed a finger on a spot on the Rio Grande. "Here." Tye studied the place Thurston had indicated.

"There's an old camp there on the Mexican side. Hasn't been used in a while though," Tye said.

"How's the shoulder?"

"Sore as hell, but it ain't keeping me from riding if that's what you are asking?" Tye answered.

"Good. I would like you to take one of your scouts and see what the hell is going on."

"When?"

"First thing in the morning. Here's a requisition for whatever supplies you think you might need for three or four days."

"Yes Sir. Anything else?" Thurston shook his head and turned to Garrison and O'Malley.

"O'Malley, I want you to start selecting a troop of fifty men. No new recruits, no inexperienced men. I've a feeling in my gut that this may be the Apache's big push to rid this land of the white man and if so, this will be a long, tough, bloody patrol and I want men that know what to expect. Lieutenant, I want you to have Captain McClellan come to my office immediately then get with the quarter master and make sure we have supplies for fifty or so men and a like number of horses available on a moments notice. I'll get with the post surgeon, Captain Schuler, to make arrangements for an ambulance and medical supplies. Mind you, this is only in case we need them. Understood?"

"Yes Sir," O'Malley and Garrison said in unison. They saluted and left. Tye and Buff were already walking back to the house.

"Seems ta kno whut he's doing."

"Who?"

"Tha Majur."

"Yeah. He's a good officer. Goes with his feelings a lot and sometimes throws the damn army manual away unlike some others I know."

"Amen to tha. Seen sum officers tha kuld not take a leek befo reeding tha manual ta make shor tha doing it rite," Buff said laughing.

"The major has given up a lot to be out here. He had a beautiful wife when he came. She was one of those ladies that had to have parties to go to, restaurants, and stores to shop. She lasted less than three months before packing up and going back to Washington. She took the heart out of Thurston, but he overcame it and has done a tremendous job out here. You have to admire him for another reason also. He came out of the War a hero and could have had a cushy job at a fort back east, but he insisted on a post on the frontier. I always respected him for that." He stopped and placed his hand on Buff's shoulder. "You go on to the house and tell Rebecca I'll be there in about an hour."

"Whar yu goin?"

"To see Dan August; one of my scouts, to tell him about leaving in the morning."

"Okay. See ya in a little while."

~~~

It was late afternoon and all the arrangements had been made just in case Tye found a need to move out quickly. The O'Malley's had invited Garrison, McClellan, Tye and Rebecca, and of course Buff to their home for coffee and cake. They all wanted to hear more stories from Buff. Master Sergeant O'Malley was Rebecca's father's brother. He was a career man and was in his mid-fifties. He was big, over six feet and broad throught the shoulders. His age had caused his middle to expand some but in a fight, he was still someone to respect. When Rebecca's father and mother had been killed, she came to Clark to live with the O'Malleys. The sergeant and his wife both thought the world of Tye. They introduced their niece to Tye and were elated when they got married. Tye had a lot of respect for them too. When he brought down the renegade, Tanza a few months ago, he rescued his good friends, the Turleys, grandson and granddaughter from the Apache Camp. The O'Malleys had taken them in as their own.

When everyone was situated Tye spoke up.

"Tell us about the Rockies, Buff. Pa always said they were hand carved by God Himself."

"Tha's not fur frum tha truth, Tye. Thos montons ar so tall tha teched tha sky. Tha are so tall that tha pines stop growing neer tha tops. In tha summur, snow never left tha tops uf them. Pine trees stud over hundert foot tall, and the aspen...tha ar God's masta piece. Tha white bark shinnen in tha sunlite and tha leeves ruslen in tha wind. Tha air wus fresh...always smeled like pinny kones. I tale yu sumthang else too...nevar knu of a man dyin uf dezese or infechion. Lots uther reesons a man culd die tho...freezing, Injuns, panthers, and whut we feered mor'n anythang else...ole ephraim."

"What do you mean by ole ephraim?" Garrison asked.
~~~

"Grizz, sonny. Meenest damn critter God ev'r did make. Seen grizz mor'n ten fut tall when uprite and way mor'n thousan pounds, claws six inchs long. When food wus scarce, a hungry wun wuld trac a man down fur food. Truth be known, problee more uf us trappr's got his self kilt by them than by injuns. Me and ole Ben damn neer wus cached in by wun wunce. Damn grizz had mine and Ben's fiftee calaber balls frum our rifles and frum our pistols in him...onlee made tha critt'r madder. Onliest thang that sav'd our sorry hides tha day wus Bridger, Fitzpatric, and Stumpy steppen in an shuting. Their bullets and ours finally stopped tha monster."

"Gitting bac to tha 'shinning montans'; tha's whut we called the Rockee Montans, sonny," he said looking at Garrison and smiling, bringing laughter from everyone including Garrison. "Tha had streems and riv'rs so cleer wun wuld thank it to be a fut deep and it wuld be five or mor fut deep. Futhur up north neer tha Yeller Stone River, wus Coulter's hell...a place liken no uther on this hear earth; hot watur shuting fiftee or hundert feet in tha air ever few minutes; pons uf hot watur bubblin; hot mud pits bubblin." He paused and took a drink of coffee and no one spoke a word. They were all ears.

"But tha main thang," he said looking at each person," wus seein places and thangs no man, at lest no white man, had seen befo." Tye nodded.

"That's what pa said...told me it was a feeling one couldn't describe. He use to tell me about the winters in the mountains and how bad they were."

"How kold do it git heer in tha wintur?" Buff asked. McClellan spoke up before anyone else.

"Pretty cold, Buff...nights may get down in twenties and daytime temps about freezing. But most of the time the cold doesn't stay but two or three days then it warms up." Buff slapped his knee and laughed.

"Hell, tha thare is Spring time tempatoors in tha Rockees," Buff chuckled. "Tematoors in tha Rockees? In tha winner ya see bout thirtee or fortee belo zero. May warm up ta zero or a little bove durin tha da. Be tha way fur weeks. Sno may be tin, twentee fut deep at times."

"My God," Garrison said. "How did you survive those conditions?"

"Bufflo robes an blankets; fur lined boots; gluves; and hats. Tha mane thang tho wus to sta dri...nev'r do nuthin tha ya mite wurk up a swet an git yurslf wet undur yur shurts and pants. Hot coffee an lots of whesky helped sum too," he added laughing. "By tha way, ya ladies wuld hav luved yur men in thos times...onlee bathed when wather allow'd...mabee wunce or twice dur'in tha winnur." He laughed, as did every one else. Rebecca, laughing, was making a face and holding her nose. She really liked this little man...and loved the way he talked.

"Pa told me he took an arrow out of your shoulder once, Buff. That right?"

"Sur 'nuff. I thank it wus in '29. We, tha's Jim, Ben, Stumpee, and me, wure trappin a small crek off'un tha Yellee Stone River. Thar wus a small island in tha middle, jus large enuf fur a kamp and fur tha horses. Plenti uf cuv'r wus thar too whut with all tha deadfalls. Man culd hide himself purty damn gud behind them thar deadfalls. Any way, we wus thru runnin our traps fur tha da and wus fleshing tha plews when Ben hollurd tha wun wurd tha all us trappr's a'feard...BLACKFUT."

"We got our guns an wus behin sum logs quiker than ya kuld spit. Tha Blackfut were in tha knee deep watur by tha time an cummin fast. Why tha didn't let luse with their arrors, I don't kno. Figured later tha wunted to kill us with knive and tomahawk cause ta do tha is big medicine to an injun. We sighted our guns. Tha wur screeming sumthang feerce...musta been bout a dozen, maybee a few mor. Any how, we eech fired them long rifles and fore uf them Blackfut dropped. Three mor wen't down when we fir'ed our pistals.

Ole Ben, he stude up, all six fut fore of himself, screeming and wavin his Bowie in wun hand and his tomeehawk in tha uther."

After a moments pause, Buff laughed, shaking his head.

"Blackfoot charging you can't be funny, Buff. " MCClellan said.

"Kno it wus'unt. I wus jus thankin abut Ben. Tha wus a sight, him standin up screeming just like them Blacfut. Thank it sort'er set them Blacfut bac fur a second.Tha Blackfut, whut wus left of'um, wus on our island with us an it wus han to han fight'n. Ben luked like a wildman. He jabb'en with that blade and swingin tha thar tomeehawk. He tuk two down imeediatly and had a third down on tha ground an wus fixin to kil him when we got sorta buzee our ownselvs and lost trac of whut wus happen'n elswhar. Anyhow, we fot'um off. Only fore or so of 'em wus able to run off but befo tha did, wun pickked up his bow that he had left on tha bank. He fired that damn arrer and it stuck me in tha sholder, tha point steekin out my bac. We knu thos Blackfut would be acomin back with sumn frends. We packed our stuf and wus gone within minutes. My sholder wud hav to wait, uther than Ben jerking tha shaff out after breking off tha point. By tha time we got our traps and found a new kamp, it wus almost dark."

"My sholder wus hurtin' sumthang feerce by tha' time. Ben, beeing tha gentlee fello he wus, pored sum whesky in tha hole in my sholder. If'n I kuda whupped him, I wuld have. Tha whesky burn sumthang feerce. Jim had a fire agoing and holden his knif in tha flames. When that blade wus red, I tuk me a deep brath and chomped down on tha peece of wud tha Ben gav me. Jim touched tha wund, front and back, melting tha skin and sealin her up. Took me abut two weeks to gane full muvement in it. Tha wus tha ferst time Ben had ta git an arrer out uf some wun, but it wusn't tha last." Pausing before continuing, he took a drink of coffee.

"Ole Bridger and me, we knu we had us a reel wildcat fur a partnur. We had sevral fites with Blackfut after that, but that wus tha onliest time I got injur'd. Ben wus hit ba two arrer's, a bullit, and sevral knife wunds ov'r tha next few yeers. Tye, yur pa became big medicin to thos Injuns ov'r tha yeers. He wus always beeing trac'd down and attaked by a Blackfut warrer trying ta make a name for himself by killin' Ben. Don't kno how many times tha tried cause Ben wusn't no braggin man. I do kno thar wus at leest five diffrent times cauz I saw them my own self...they were dedder than a peece uf wud. Another man, Liver Eating Johnson, had tha same thang happen to him a few yeers later. Tha Crow killed his injun wife an ten yeer ole son. He teaked them down an killed all six uf them and tore their livers out. Wurd got out he ate tha livers and tha Crow gave him tha name, Liver Eater. For mor'n twenty years a Crow warrior, trying to make a anme fur hisself, would try to kill him. Don't kno how manee tried but it wus mor'n a few. Heered wun time it wus mor'n forty, but I don't kno fur certain.Tha finally gave up an made peece with Johnson."

"When I heard you were at Tye's and Rebecca's," McClellan said, "I found an old book about the mountain men in my drawer that had put there a long time ago ...you know, one of those dime novels that were popular back east."

Shakespeare laughed. "Written by sum greener like Lootenant Garrison that ne'r been anywhar close ta tha montons." Everyone laughed.

"I know what you mean, Buff, but this guy had actually interviewed this man named Parkman that supposedly had been there trapping. Anyway, one of the things he said that got my attention was on the first page. "I defy anyone to defy that there was no life more perilous than that of a mountain man." He went on to describe the daily life of one. If you had to sum up what it was like, what would you say?"

"Don't reckon I kno'wd that feller but I figerr he's rite abut that. Don't kno much abut city life but if'n wun lives and works in one his life is prettee safe excepting fur mabee sickness. A soldur has to wurry abut who he's gonna fite killin him. A mountain man...well he has ta wurry abut lots of thangs such as: freezing ta death, starving ta death, Grizzly, packs uf wolves, and Injuns. Hell, up in thos montons in winter, a simple broke leg kuld kill a man." He stood up and continued because his back was beginning to hurt sitting.

"A monton man's life wusn't skuduled by tha kalendar. He worked when tha wether allowed him ta work. Frum November ta March, sumtimes April, tha streems wur froze over. Tha Spring wus tha most profitable time ta trap cauz the furs wur thicker after tha wintur. Wintur was bad mainly becauz of bordom. Thar wusn't much a man kud do when its thirtee belo zero and twentee fut of snow."

"Always wondered what all a trapper had to have to survive in those mountains? McClellan asked.

"A trappr didn't have a lot uf personal stuff: Usually a horse to ride, an if'n he's lucky, a pak horse too, a saddle blanket and saddle, a sak with his trapps, extra moccskins, powder, bait fur tha beever, tobbaca, flint and steel fur making a fire in it. On his own self, he had shirt and pants made uf smoked buffalo skin, leggings, a heavy buffalo robe, a hat, and strips uf skin ta wrap around his moccskins to help keep his feet warm and dry. He wud have a belt with a nife, tomeehawk and pistol. He wud have his rifle in a fur sheeth across his lap. I had me two mor pistols on my saddle. He wud trade fur coffee, flour, salt, powder, an lead at tha rondavu we had eech summer. If'n he wus lucky, he wud walk away with sum muney also. I guess wun cud say excpting fur trying ta keep fum starving, freezing, getting eaten by grizz, getting scalped by the Blackfoot, an half dozen uther thangs tha kud happen, our way uf life was pretee boring." Everyone got a good laugh from that statement.

Mrs. O'Malley stood up. "It's getting to be late for us old folks, so we had better call it a day." She held out her hand, and Sergeant O'Malley, taking it, stood up. Garrison and Delacruz both stood up and offered their thanks for a pleasant evening.

"Befo ya'll leve," Shakespeare said. "I waunt eech uf ya to kno wun thang." Everyone had stopped and was giving Buff their full attention. Buff put his hand on Tye's shoulder. "When I ferst saw Tye, I wus sur I wus lookin at a ghost. He's tha spitten imege uf his pa. Frum whut I hear, he has tha bark on jus like Ben." He looked at Garrison. "Tha's montane man talk, sonny. Meens he is corageous, a man wun kuld depend on in a tite. Ben wus tha brav'st man I ev'r knu. I figer Tye's just like him. Kno I ain't tellin ya anythang ya don't kno but jus thought Tye shuld kno... he's jus like his pa." He turned and shook Tye's hand. "Jus lik'um." He repeated.

Sergeant O'Malley spoke up. "You're right, Buff. We all have had our butts saved by him; some of us more than once."

It was a beautiful fall night as the three of them walked to their house. They stopped for a minute to admire the stars that were shining like diamonds without the light of the moon to take their beauty away.

"Pretty ain't they, Buff." Tye said.

"Luk as pretee as tha did in tha montons. Nev'r get tired uf luking at them." As they entered the house Tye turned to Buff.

"We'll see you in the morning, Buff. Goodnight." Buff was thinking this here being liked, maybe even loved, could grow on a man as he walked to his room.

~~~

Well before daylight, Shakespeare dressed and walked outside on the porch. He damned near jumped out of his skin when Tye spoke.

"Morning Buff."

"Gawdamighty, Tye. Ya dam nea'r skared me ta deth. Wha ya do'n out heer this eerly?"

"Always been an early riser, Buff. Gotta meet my scout in a few minutes and hit the trail."
~~~

"Glad ya ar a earlee rizer, Tye, but I'll tal ya sumthang. If'n I had me a wife tha luks like Rebecca, tha onliest way wun culd git me outa bed wuld be with a stic uf dynimite." Tye laughed with him.

"She's as nice as she is pretty, Buff. Can't tell you how lucky I am to have her." Rebecca's voice startled both of them.

"Well, Buff, what he said goes both ways. I'm pretty lucky too." She came out on the porch in a robe and hugged Buffs neck and kissed Tye.

"Morning honey," she said.

"If'n tha don't beet all. Tha youn'un gets tha kiss an tha ole man jus gits a hug."

"Well we can fix that." Rebecca said. She stepped over and gave him another hug and added a kiss on the cheek.

"Now what are you two doing out here? It's cold out here. Come on inside and I'll make some coffee." They followed her inside.

"No time, honey. I gotta go. Dan will be waiting."

"How long will you be gone?"

"Couple or three days."

"Be careful, honey," she whispered hugging his neck.

"Always am. Take care of her, Buff."

"Yu can kount on it, Tye"

Chapter Three

Tye and Dan had traveled all day to get to the spot Thurston had indicated on the map. It was no problem finding it when they got close as all one had to do was follow the sound of the drums. BOOM boom boom boom BOOM boom boom boom BOOM...it was a monotonous beat, always a one hundred eighty beats per minute and never changing. The land they traveled through was desolate country. It was an arid land and showed no mercy to the unwary traveler. As far as one could see it was sand, rocks, and rattlesnakes. Except around the water holes, the largest trees were the thorny chapparal. The land was full of life if one would take time to look for it. To Tye and Dan, it was home and they loved it. It was full dark when they made camp on the Texas side of the river.

The Apache camp was just across the river in Mexico. There were several fires but impossible to tell how many braves were there, but one could tell there were more than a few.

"You want first watch or second?" Tye asked Dan.

"First."

"Then wake me in four hours. Tye scooted back down the slope to camp and spread his bedroll. It was strange that the drums, after you got used to them, were no deterrent to sleep. He was sleeping soundly in a few minutes...at least as sound as a man always living on the edge could.

~~~
~~~

The sun was just starting its' trek across the Texas sky as Tye lay on his stomach looking down on the largest Apache ranchero he had ever seen. Lying beside him was Dan.

"I never would have believed it." Tye said softly as they watched the braves milling around. "I can't believe the Lipans have this many warriors in one ranchero."

"They must be fifty or more." Dan replied with Tye barely hearing his soft spoken words above the sound of the Apache drums. As they watched, another band of twenty or so Apaches rode into the ranchero and was received by much shouting and celebrating.

"What the hell is going on Tye?" Dan asked. "That last bunch is Chiricahuas."

"Beats the hell out of me; I've never seen Chiricahua and the Lipan together before, but I'll tell you one thing for sure, it ain't good news for us or the people living on the border... on both sides of the river. They ain't getting together for just a friendly powwow, I'll guarantee you that."

Tye and Dan took turns watching the rest of the day. While one watched, the other was back down the hill where the horses were, trying to sleep. Sleep was hard to come by because of the drums which were much louder now. They didn't think there was much danger right now as the Rio Grande separated them and the Apache ranchero and there had been no reports of any Apaches in the area on this side of the river. Besides, at this point of the river, sixty to seventy foot high bluffs that ran for five miles or more in both directions prevented any crossing of the Rio Grande. The river had carved its way thru these rocks over thousands of years and there was no bank to walk on. The water touched the cliffs, and it ran deep in some places and too swift in others to cross.

Major Thurston had told Tye that the new Indian Agent reported to him that it looked like some of the young bucks had left the. Joe Fisher, the new agent, seemed like an honest man to Tye. The previous agent, a man named Taggert, had been as crooked as a snake and caused many deaths, both white and red, by his starving of the Apaches. Tye had been instrumental in bringing down and killing Taggert and bringing in his partner, a man named Meecham. Meecham was now serving ten to twenty years in prison along with his men. They had been keeping most of the cattle and other provisions the government had been sending for the Apaches, selling them and lining their pockets.

Tye was resting when he was surprised to hear Dan calling his name. He was up in an instant and making his way back up the hill the short distance to where Dan was.

"What's going on Dan?"

"Take a look and you tell me what you see." Dan said nodding toward the ranchero. Tye scrambled up the few more feet that it took to get to the cliff overlooking the ranchero. He could not believe what he saw.

"What the hell!" He exclaimed. "Where did they all come from?" Tye asked.

"A large bunch came in a few minutes ago." Dan answered. "Couple of smaller groups appeared about thirty minutes ago. Look at the last group."

Tye holding his hand over the field glasses to prevent the now setting sun from reflecting off the lens looked the last bunch over. He lowered the glasses and turned to look at Dan.

"I don't believe it Dan. I just can't believe it." He repeated. "That last bunch is Mescaleros and if my eyes ain't lying, that's Loco leading them."

He took the glasses and looked again. "There are over two hundred and fifty Apaches down there and not a single kid or squaw."

"They ain't planning a party for us, I guarantee you that." Dan stated.

"What bothers me is how in hell this many warriors can be off the reservations and no one reporting it?"

They continued their watch the rest of the day with only a couple of smaller bands arriving. Tye was taxing his brain trying to figure out why they would be coming together like this. How in hell the Lipan, Mescaleros, White Mountain Apache, and Chiricahuas, and who else knows, could get together. Hell, there's even a few Tontos' and Warm Springs Apaches among them. They have never done that before. They always fought their separate wars. They were all Apaches but have never helped each other against the whites or the Mexicans, or even against raiding Kiowa's or Comanche. He was totally bumfuzzled for the first time in his life. Meanwhile, the damn drums continued their rhythmic beat.

Later, as the sun was passing below the tops of the hills the drums changed their beat; they got even louder and faster, raising the curiosity for both Tye and Dan. As they watched, the Apaches who had been simply milling around and mingling with each other seemed to be getting organized. A large circle was being formed by the braves with a fire burning in the center. Three men were in the center by themselves. All of a sudden the drums stopped and it was so quiet, it startled a man. You could hear the water running in the river sixty feet below where Tye and Dan lay. One of men in the center of the ring stood up and began to speak. His voice was carrying to where they lay but not enough that they could understand every word that was being said.

"That's Juh-nah speaking, he's the big dog with the Lipan," Dan said.

~~~

Juh-nah raised his arms toward the darkening sky and looked around at the faces of the braves that circled him. The fire was making shadows dance across their faces as they sat Indian style, legs crossed, elbows resting on their knees, eagerly waiting on Juh-nah's words.
~~~

"One moon ago I had a vision." He paused as a murmur went around the fire. Indians of all tribes were big believers in visions and a warrior who had one was thought to be touched by the Great Spirit. "In my vision I saw my father and my grandfather. I saw your fathers and grandfathers. They were not Lipan, Mescaleros, White Mountain, or Chiricahuas. They were Apaches. They were as one and they possessed strength. In my vision I saw many pony soldiers and they were all dead, killed by this strength. We are all Apaches and we can defeat our enemies if we are as one. This is the reason I sent runners to all the tribes to meet here on this day. My brothers, the time has come to either drive the white man out of our country or....." He was stopped by a tremendous cascade of shouts and even some firing of guns. He raised his arms again and the noise ceased and he continued. "Or decide to live side by side with them in peace." This statement was followed by complete silence.

He looked around and said. "Never, not in our time, our father's times, nor in their father's time have all Apaches come together to talk as we do now. Is there one of us who has not lost a brother, mother, father, or friend to the guns of the bluecoats. I think not. As Chief of the Lipan, I have lost many relatives and many more friends to them. No one has fought them longer or more fearlessly than the Lipan. But I tell you now, the white men are like the stars in the sky, too many to count. They never run out of bullets. They have the long guns on wheels that can kill from great distances. It is death for our people to continue the fight if each fights alone. We must band together and fight as one if we are to drive the whites out of our land." This was followed again by much shouting and show of support.

Another of the men in the center stood up and raised his arms and everyone quieted down, for this man was a man they all respected, not that they didn't Juh-nah, but Juh-nah was old and no longer a war chief. This man was a warrior they all knew. His name was Loco. The only Apache, who was better known than he, was Cochise.

"We have come together from great distances to talk; some from Arizona and some from Mexico. Others from Texas have come. What my friend, Juh-nah, says is true. The white man is like the stars." He bent down and picked up a handful of dirt and let it slowly sift from his hand. "They are like the grains of sand, too many to count." He picked up another handful. "This is our land. This was our fathers land and our grandfathers land. Now, the white man wants to own the land. They think the only good Apache is a dead Apache and it makes no difference if it is warrior, woman, or child. This is in their papers that are handed out. I had a friend tell me what the written words were and that is what they say. Juh-nah is old and wise and what he says is true. I ask you, had you rather live as a beggar on a reservation until you are old or had you rather fight for your land and live free, if even for a short time." Guns firing and braves jumping up and screaming showed him their answer. He raised his arms again and the noise ceased and they all sat down again.

Loco continued. "I and my people had rather live free, as an Apache warrior for a short time, than live a long life taking handouts from the white man. We will fight until there is no more of our blood to spill." Again, much celebrating followed his speech. Among the many young warriors listening were some who would in later years cause much havoc among the whites. There was Nanah, Victoria, To-say, and of course, Goyahkla, who had already had a reputation as a white hater. The Mexicans named him Geronimo. He stood up and walked to the center of the ring of warriors.

"I agree with what Juh-nah and Loco have said. I and my people will not live like beggars. We will fight for our land and our way of life to the last man. The white man does not want peace. If we say we will live where he wants us to and they find the yellow rock there, we have to leave. Wherever they want us to go and we go, they will eventually make us go somewhere else, by force. We have heard your voices and we know your feelings. The chiefs and medicine men will make smoke tonight and make plans. We will speak again when the sun is high." Guns were firing and the night was filled with Apache shrieks. Then, the steady beating of the drums began again and the warriors were dancing to the rhythmic beat.

Tye and Dan had decided that there was going to be hell to pay and would start back in the morning to report to Thurston." First watch or second?" Tye asked.

"First, again" Dan answered. Tye made his way back to the horses and walked over to his horse, Sandy. He was a gift from Thurston for his part in bringing down the vicious Vazquez gang a couple months earlier. He was a gelding and bigger than the average horse, being about seventeen hands tall. This was good as Tye was six foot two and one hundred ninety pounds of solid muscle. He was a strikingly handsome man with his long, black hair and matching mustache. His steel blue eyes were clear and it was said he could see as well as a turkey buzzard which was damn good. His skin was dark from years of being under the Texas sun. His torso looked like it was chisled from granite. He had lived all of his twenty nine years here on the Border. He was the best known scout in this part of Texas and was feared by the bandits and respected by the Apaches. When he was with the Rangers, he had tracked down so many bandits they had put a bounty on him at one time. He always wore his knee high Apache moccasin boots, faded blue cavalry pants and cavalry hat, along with his buckskin shirt. The shirt had been his fathers; he had it on the day he died. The shirt was made by his mother and he would never part with it. He had a 10" Bowie in his right boot, a pistol on his hip and carried a Sharps rifle.

He gave Sandy some oats and water and then lay down for a couple of hours before relieving Dan. Before going to sleep though, his thoughts, as always, drifted toward his new wife Rebecca. They had been married about two months earlier and he was happier now than he had ever been in his life. His only regret was that his mother and father never got to meet her. He knew they would have loved her as he did. He was a grown man and was well know as meaner than a rattler in a fight. He was all man, mucho hombre as the Mexicans would say, but when he was alone though, as now, and thinking about his parents, it always brought a lump to his throat.

His dad had taught him every thing as far as fighting, whether it is with fist, knives, tomahawks, or guns. At fifteen, Tye could whip most grown men and by the time he was eighteen, no one could best him in a standup, knockdown bare knuckle fight. He was an expert with a Bowie and had already killed several Apaches with one. He could live off the land as well as an Apache and could travel on foot almost as well. He could track and read sign as well as any Apache, better than most. The bandits said he could track a lizard over rocks and if he got on your trail, you were as good as caught. He knew all the water holes, hideouts, blind canyons, and even the places where the Rio Grande could and could not be crossed. Plus, Tye had the one thing that his father had but few others had an extra sense that allowed him to 'feel' trouble before it happened. No patrol he had scouted for had ever been ambushed. He fell asleep listening to the constant, monotonous beat, thinking of Rebecca and glad Buff was there to watch over her.

Tye woke up suddenly as a rock moved ever so slightly. Dan was making his way down the hill to wake Tye up. Years of living out here makes a man sleep light and any noise that is not a normal night sound will wake him immediately. If it doesn't, he might not wake up. He was putting his boots on when Dan got to him.

Dan was laughing. "What's so funny?" Tye asked.

"Nothing is funny. I was doing my best to injun up on you and not wake you. Shouda knowed better."

"Anything going on at the ranchero?" Tye asked.

"Nope. No more has come in that I can tell. All seem to be asleep except the damn drummers."

For the first time since waking, Tye was aware of the drums beating. Strange, he thought, how a man could tune out the drums but a rock making a slight noise could wake him up. He stood up and started up the hill to stand his watch. It was about midnight. He would wake Dan up about three a.m. and head back to Clark and report to Thurston.

Chapter Four

The early morning sun, looking like a great orange ball just beginning its trek across the sky, found Tye and Dan half way back to Fort Clark. They were now on the Old Mail Road and making good time. Tye figured they should be there by late morning. There had been little talk between the two men as both were tired, riding on less than three hours sleep. Both were anxious to report and then see their wives and in Dans' case, also his kids. Tye, as tired as he was, was thinking of what he had seen at the ranchero and was struggling to come up with an answer as to what was going on. He was sure of one thing only, it wasn't good.

~~~

A pipe was being passed around the small group of braves inside the wickiup, each taking a smoke and then tilting their heads back and blowing the smoke into the air. After each had smoked, Jun-nah spoke.

"Each of you heard our peoples' voices last night. They want war and drive the intruders out of our land. We must decide what we are going to do, how we are going to do it, and when we are going to do it."

Loco spoke up. "My people are ready now. My hesitation is only because in a short time, maybe two moons, the cold winds will be blowing in the high country where we live and it gets much colder than here, where we are now."

"I feel the same way," said Goyahkla. "We can use the time between now and when the warm winds come again to
~~~

make small raids and increase our supply of guns and bullets."

"We can use the time to gather food and place it in areas where our women and children can go and be safe," said Na-tay-yah, the Lipan medicine man. "This would be good, to wait until after the cold." Na-tay-yah was old; almost sixty winters had come and gone since he was born. He was respected for his wisdom by all Lipans and even Goyahkla and Loco knew of him. He was known as a man of visions and great magical power. "Myself and the medicine men of the other tribes can speak with the great spirits and learn of their wishes to help make our decisions."

Jun-nah stood up followed by the others. "It is decided then. We are all of the same mind. We will wait until the warm air flows from the south before we attack and drive out the white man. Myself and the Lipan's along the Texas and Mexico border, Goyahkla and Loco in Mexico and Arizona. If we all begin at the same time the bluecoats will be spread over too great an area and they will be easier to defeat. We will speak of this tonight with our people. They will be happy that we are going to fight as their fathers did." He looked at each man in the wickiup. "If we do this together we may win. If one of us does not, it will be the end of our way of life...the end of the Apache."

Loco spoke up. "This is a great day for our people. We will break out the tiwsin and drink and dance tonight in celebration of our coming victory."

~~~

Back at Fort Clark headquarters, Thurston was being entertained by Shakespeare and his stories of the days of the mountain man and the 'shinning times' as he so often referred to them. He liked this old man even though he didn't believe half of the words that came out of his mouth. Hell, he couldn't understand half of them. There was not a single thing about
~~~

him that would distinguish him from the next man but you could tell he was one tough old hombre. His eyes shone bright for a man his age and as he so eloquently stated, "Theese ole eyes done seen thangs ya only read abut in them tha'r books. Land no white man see'd befor'. Montans with streems so cleer and kold ya culdn't bathe even in tha summ'r without frezzn' yur butt off'n." Thurston was also amazed how Buff moved. No way would his body movements tell you they belonged to a seventy plus year old man.

His tales were interrupted by the orderly saying that Tye was back. Thurston jumped up and started toward the door.

"Back! Back so soon." He said to himself as he headed to the door. Shakespeare stood up and stepped aside as Thurston passed.

"Morning Major." Tye said shaking his hand and then the Major was shaking Dans' hand.

"Glad you boys are back. I'm anxious to hear about those drums."

"Howdy, Buff." Tye said, then turning toward Thurston. "You got damn good reason to worry Major. There were over two hundred fifty braves at that council."

"TWO HUNDRED FIFTY." Thurston blurted out loudly. “That’s hard to believe. Are you sure?"

"Dammitt, Major that's what you pay me for. Do you think I would make something like that up?” Tye asked angrily.

Thurston put his hand on the desktop and sorter held himself up. "I didn't mean it that way Tye. I'm sorry. You know how I feel about you. It's just hard....God, Two hundred and fifty."

"That ain't all major." Dan said. “You ain't heard the good part."

"What does he mean?" Thurston asked looking at Tye.

"Well major, you had the Lipans, Mescalero, Chiricahuas, and even White Mountain Apaches, all in one ranchero, making talk."

"Wh...What kind of talk?" Thurston asked.

"Don't know Major, couldn't hear all that was said but I promise you they weren't talking about giving the white man early Christmas presents." Then Tye added, "Unless it would be a basket with his head in it. Dan and I have been trying to figure things out since last night. The only thing I can come up with is by coming together their strength would over whelm us here or at some other part of the country, maybe Arizona or Mexico."

Shakespeare had been quiet, standing in the background, but now blurted out. "Ya kno, thos injuns kuld jus be getten thar bisness lined up with eech uther. Seed it befo."

"I'm sorry Mr. McDovitt." An embarrassed Thurston said. "I forgot my manners. Dan August, this is Shakespeare McDovitt." They shook hands.

"Tye's been telling me about you," Dan said.

"My frends call me 'Buff'". He said.

"What are you talking about, Apaches getting their business lined up?" Thurston asked.

"Don't no these heer paches' but I figger thar like all uther injuns I fite agan all my life. Thay ain't gonna fite togather but bye all atackin at sam time in eech wuns homelands, they jus mite spread ya solder' boy a mite thin acros this hear cuntre."

Nothing was said for a moment then Tye spoke up. "I never thought of it that way, but you may be right. I really can't see them fighting side by side and all under one war chief. I can see them planning their attacks to coincide with one another. That sure as hell would prevent the forts from sending soldiers to help other forts."

"I'm getting dispatches out to Fort Duncan, Fort Inge, and Camp Verde now." Thurston said sitting down in his chair and getting out writing paper. "I'll send another to the District Commander in San Antonio and he can advise the District Commander in Arizona and New Mexico. Now, I know you and Dan are anxious to see your wives and I know for certain you," Looking at Tye, "Have a lot to talk about with 'Buff' here. I'll see you later or in the morning." He stood up and shook all three men's hands and sat back down and hollered for his orderly to find his Adjutant.

Outside, Tye and Dan shook hands saying they would see each other the next morning. Dan took Tye's horse, Sandy, along with his horse to the stables.

~~~

As they approached his home, Tye saw Rebecca sweeping off the porch. He whistled and when she saw him, came running to him throwing herself into his arms, kissing him at the same time.

"Tha's whut I call a welcum." Shakespear said, laughing loudly." Yessur, a reel welcum."

Rebecca and Tye laughed as they walked into the house

As soon as they sit down, Tye asked. "Where were we before I left on patrol?"

"Jus talkin abut yur pa and me in tha montons the ferst cuple yeers."

Tye and Rebecca sat on the porch enjoying the fall afternoon listening to Buff tell about Ben's first experience with trap robbers.

"We, that's Jim, Ben, Absher, and me, wus lying on tha bedrolls rond tha fire talking bout tha day's reesults. It wus still kold as hell as it wus late March or early April and thar wus still lots uf sno in these high montons uf tha Rockees. Ben, Absner, and Jim had dun dam gud that day, but me, I had nuthen even tho my traps had dun been sprung. Jim sade he'd seed this befor. Damn trappr's too laze to set their own traps and make thar living running uther mens' traps. Ben asked whut we wus going ta do abut it. I answered him in no uncertain terms. Whut tha hell ya think wa do sunny, we keel tha sumbitches," I tol him matter of factly. Ben, being tha
~~~

pelgrim he wus, tho't that wus a little survere. Jim xplained ta him tha 'Law of tha Monton Man.' Everywun knos tha consiquences uf runnin anuther mans trap line. Tha wuldn't be tha ferst ta pay. Ben sade he understud tha have ta pay; but kill them? I told him I no ya ar nu out hear, but ler'n won thang ar ya ain't gonna make it out hear I tol him. No matt'r whut ya have herd bout us monton men, we ar honust and won't stan fer steeling, specilly frum each othur. We jus slap them on the han, thay jus muve to sumone else's trap line, mabee keel sum por trapper ev'n. Ole Jim, he laughed and told Ben tha I puts thangs pretee short and ta tha point. He tol Ben, he'd seed this befor and wunce tha steeling starts, tha don't stop til somewun is hurt or kilt. Best ta stop this rite now; befor tha happens ta a honust trapper. Ben, he thought fur a minut and then sade he understud. Buff paused for a moment, getting his thoughts together.

"Jim xplaned ta Ben tha it's not like we are gonna line them up and shut them. When yu katch them, tha usually fite and then it's yu or them. Saw ole Ben shrugg his sholdurs. Tol me he had a lot ta lurn out heer. It wus quiet fur a few moments as we lay thar luking at tha stars. Ole Ben ya no, he nev'r tired uf duing tha. Tha kold monton air wus kleerer than on tha plains whar he wus raised. Them thar stars, wa'll thay twinkled lik diamouns on a black cloth when thar wus no moon lightin' up tha sky. He tol me sevral times how much he loved this cuntry, tha snow kapped montons, tha tall trees that in places wus so thick a man kudn't walk in a straight line fur more than three or four steps. Then thar wus tha aspens, tha most beetifull tree God ever kreated whut with thar white bark shining in tha moonlite. Thar wus tha kold streems and tha places whare tha ground wus hot yeer round and hot watur gushed into tha air ever few minites. It wus a awsum plac ta live and ain't no way a man kud live here and not kno fur certan that thar had to be a God to kreate such a place as this heer Yellerston."

Tye interupted Buff. "I been trying to remember but can't ever remember pa mentioning a man named Jerome Absher trapping with ya'll."

"Did yur pa ev'r menshud a man named Stumpee?"

"Sure...quite a bit."

"Wal, Stumpy and Absher ar tha same. I think I tol yu abut Ben givin niknames to peeple."

"Oh yeah, he was the tall skinny man."

"Ole Jerome hated tha handle his parents gave him. He wus tall, mabee little ove'r six fut and skinee as a aspen. Seemed sorta nat'ral Ben sade that he shud be kalled Stumpy. He wus Stumpy frum then on. Ben wus gud at that...giv'in peeple niknames. Tol ole Stump tha he wud nev'r have ta wurry abut getting himself shot by tha Blackfut cause he wus to damn skinee ta hit.. I'll tell yu wun thang, Stumpy wus a man to ride tha riv'r with. He tawked tu much sumtimes an we had ta shut him up but we wus gud frens. He saved my tale mor'n wunce in fites with tha Blackfut. Remember wunce we had been ambushed by tha damn Blackfut and while runnin our horses ta git away, my horse went down, shot plum full of arrors. Ole Stump, he culd hav gottun safly away but came bac ta git me. He tuk an arror in tha sholdur duing it. Yeah, he wus wun ta hav as a fren."

"Did you catch the men running your traps?" Tye asked. Buff threw up his hands.

"If'n all yu ar thru askin questions, I'll git bac ta my story." Rebecca snickered bringing a quick glance and a smile from Tye.

~~~

As Buff was entertaining Tye and Rebecca, the Cates brothers, Yancey and Billy, entered Brackett and headed for the larger of the two saloons. They were ex-conferdrate soldiers who had ridden with Quantrill. They continued their killing with Quantrill's raiders even after the war. They hated
~~~

the Union Army, they hated the government, and they hated the laws set up by the government. They made their own laws as they traveled. They had escaped a hanging in San Antonio only because Jake Plummer and Jared Robinson, also ex-confederate soldiers who rode with Quantrill, broke them out of jail. They had picked up some more men, Mexicans, who were also inclined to rob and kill rather than do a honest days work. Jake and Jared entered the town from the opposite direction and headed for the same saloon. Over the next thirty minutes, Juan and Alfonso Cortez followed the same plan as did the three other members of the Cates gang...all coming in one or two at a time and entering the same saloon. Once inside they sat at different tables, trying to blend in with the afternoon crowd. A few minutes after everyone settled down Yancey stood up and in a loud voice.

"EVERYONE LET ME HAVE YOUR ATTENTION." Things got as quite as a Church with everyone wondering what was happening. Yancy continued in a normal voice. "If all of you would be so kind as to drop your guns w..."he didn't finish.

"You going to make us all by yourself, you bastard," an old man said going for his gun. He was shot by Billy from behind and all hell broke loose. These customers were not going to lie down and be robbed. More went for their guns as did Jim, the saloon owner, who reached under the bar and came up with a pistol. Two bullets from Yancy cut him down. Two troopers, who came in at the wrong time from across the creek at Fort Clark, were gunned down by Billy and Jake. Other members of the gang opened fire and two more patrons dropped before the rest dropped their guns and stood, with their hands in the air. They were lined up against the wall and their money taken. All the cash was taken off the tables and Yancey took the cash from the cash drawer.

"CROWD GATHERING OUTSIDE," Lupe Ortiz hollered.

"LET'S GO." Yancey ordered in a loud voice. When they hit the door, they fired their guns in the air, scattering the confused crowd. Mounting their horses, they stormed out of Brackett, heading west on the Old Mail Road.

~~~

Captain Delacruz, along with three troopers, were running across the bridge into Brackett at the same time the outlaws were leaving. Grabbing the first civilian he came to he screamed. "WHAT THE HELL IS GOING ON?"

"Dunno." the man said. He looked toward the saloon. "Something happened in the saloon. Was a lot of shots fired."

"Let's go." Delacruz said to his men.

There was total chaos inside.

"EVERYONE STAND STILL," he ordered. Things got quite. "All you men stand aside and let me see what's going on." Several men stared talking at once. "QUITE." he shouted and it was quickly so quite you could hear a pin drop. Delacruz couldn't believe the mess, bodies everywhere and lots of blood. "Shit," he said when he seen the two troopers. Then he saw Jim. "Dammitt to hell. Get this man on the bar." he ordered two men. They picked up Jim who was still alive despite two wounds. Delacruz turned to one of his men. "Get the hell over to headquarters and get Thurston over here then go get Tye. Get sawbones over here too."

"Old Sawbones is here, Captain." Captain McAlister, post surgeon, said coming in behind Delacruz.

"This man is still breathing." Delacruz said, pointing to the bar where Jim was. McAlister hurried over telling Delacruz to check the others that were lying scattered around the saloon.

"Do what you have to do to save this man, Doc. He's a good friend of mine and every other soldier at the fort... and especially Tye."
~~~

~~~

"Whal, like I wus saying fore ya started askin tha questions. Ev'erwun had a passle uf beevers 'ceptin me. I had nune even tho ev'er damn trap had been sprung. Old Jim now, he wus mor pashunt than this heer old boy. I wus plum reedy to kill sumwun but old Jim tol me ta reelax...set my traps tumorrow as usual and see if'n tha theef cumes bac. Weel deal with it then, he said. Nex day I dune jus that and aftur Jim set his'n, he joined me, hidden whar we culd see sum uf my traps. Well, about noon..." he was interupted by a knock on the door. Tye answered it.

"DO WHAT! Who shot him?" He turned to Rebecca and Buff who was wondering what was going on. "Jim's been shot." Tye said. Rebecca ran to him and hugged him.

"Is...Is he dead?"

"Not yet. At least not a few minutes ago. Buff, please stay here with Rebecca. I'll be back as soon as I can." He left at a dead run with the trooper toward town.

"Whu's Jim?"

"Tye's friend who owns the saloon." Rebecca said, wiping her tears with the palm of her hand.

"Tha's tha feller tha I furst met when I kame in nite fore last. Tuk me ta Tye's old quaters to sleep in." He shook his head. "A reel frendly feller."

~~~

Major Thurston arrived at Jim's place and was apalled. He walked over to where Delacruz was watching McAlister work on Jim. "How's he doing, Captain?"

"He'll be down a long time but old sawb...uh, excuse me, Sir. I mean Captain McAlister says he'll live. He took two bullets...one high in the chest and one in the shoulder. He has the bullet out of his chest; fixing to go after the one in the shoulder."

"Tye been told yet?" Thurston asked, knowing Jim and Tye were close friends.

"I'm here, Major." Tye said coming in the door. "What happened?" he asked looking at his friend, then at the others lying on the floor. "They all dead?"

"Yes," Delacruz answered. "All we know for sure is that several men came in to rob Jim and all the men that were in here. Old Bob over there wasn't going to give up his gun and when he pulled it out to use it, all hell broke loose."

"How many are dead?" Thurston asked.

"Five, counting the two soldiers."

"Soldiers?" Tye questioned.

"Two troopers who were off duty, come in at the wrong time to have a drink with Jim." Delacruz said. Tye walked over to the two men. He knew their faces but not their names. They had been on patrols wth him before. "Which way did they go?"

"West, Tye. Hell bent fur lether," said someone from the crowd.

"Two of them were the Cates brothers." said another.

"You know them?" Tye asked spotting the man in the crowd.

"Nope, just saw them a couple months ago in San Antonio. They were gonna be hung for murder and horse stealing. Guess they escaped. They are pure poison I hear. Don't think nuthing about killing someone." Tye turned to Thurston.

"How quick can you get a patrol together?"

"Under the circumstances, we'll bypass the paper work...maybe thirty minutes." Tye picked up a piece of paper and scribbled some names. "Can you get these men and four or five seasoned troopers?" Thurston looked at the names, nodded his head. He gave the list to Delacruz.

"Get these men immediately. Have Sergeant Major O'Malley pick six good men to accompany Tye and the others.

I'll get to the quartermaster and get supplies for ten men and horses for...how long, Tye?"

"Week, Major."

"Get to it, Captain. I'm headed to the quartermaster, Tye. See you at the stables in thirty minutes," Thurston said as he left.

Tye moved over to the bar and put his hand on Jim's forehead. "You sure he's going to be alright, Doc?"

"He'll make it, Tye. One inch lower and it would have been all over." "Thanks, Doc. See you in a few minutes, Major."

Chapter Five

Tye had said his goodbyes to Rebecca and told Buff how glad he was that he was here to take care and watch over her. Outside, he told Buff all the details of what happened in the saloon.

"My God. How kan sum men be kold bluded killers like tha is beyond this old feller's undurstandin." Buff said. "Yu bes be on yer toes, Tye. This kud be worser than trackin Injuns."

"Got a feeling it's going to get bloody, Buff. Just take care of Rebecca."

"Dun, Tye. Now git goin...be karful."

"Always am, Buff." He shook the old man's hand firmly and left, knowing Buff would die protecting her.

~~~

"Santo's coming," Billy said looking back over his shoulder.

"Bout damn time," said Yancey, turning in his saddle to take a look. "Hold up a minute," he said to his men. The rest stopped, all looking back at the rider coming. They had been riding hard since the killing and robbery in Brackett and the horses needed a breather anyway.

"Think he's spotted anyone trailing us, Yance?" asked Plummer while rolling a smoke.

"I doubt it. It'll take the stupid army half a day to get a patrol on our trail." Juan and Alfonso Cortez both laughed at the same time. Yance looked hard at them.
~~~

"What's so damn funny?"Both men stopped laughing.

"Apparently, you don't know what the hell you are talking about," Juan stated. Yancey reached for his gun but was stopped by Billy grasping his arm.

"DON'T NO ONE TALK TO ME LIKE THAT," yelled Yancey still trying to get to his gun. Billy held fast.

"Calm down, Yance...just calm the hell down for a second." Billy said. Yancey relaxed a little but if looks could kill, Juan would be lying on the ground for the varmits to pick his bones. "What do you mean by that?" Billy asked Juan.

"Fort Clark ain't like other forts around here. This here fort has a commanding officer that is tough and gets things done in a hurry. They have this scout named Watkins that's eight foot tall and meaner than a snake; he can track better than an Apache; he can live off the land like they do; he can dissappear and then appear again at will; his horse is bigger any horse in the country and is faster than the wind; once Watkin...". He was interrupted by Yancey.

"What in hell's bells you talking about, Mex?" Yancey asked. "Ain't no man like that."

"My brother exaggerated some...but not much," Alfonso stated. "I saw him once. Ain't eight foot tall but he's over six foot and built like a blacksmith. He's brought down so many outlaws that a bounty was put on his head by bandits along the Border...no one collected. He is the one who captured the Vasquez gang two or three months ago."

"Heard about that,"said Plummer.

"Well, you can bet your ass that he is on our trail right now." said Juan.

"He's like the damn army," Yancey said. "Him and the soldiers will be firing the single shot sharps and we'll be firing our thirteen shot Henrys...ain't going to be much of a fight I'd say."

"Maybe not, if you can see him to shoot that repeater at," Lupe said. Santos rode up at that time in a cloud of choking, white dust.

"See anyone following us?" Yancey asked. Santos took a drink from his canteen, wiping his mouth with a dirty sleeve.

"No one, Senor. No one is close."

"No one is close! What the hell does that mean? Is someone following us or not?" Yancey demanded.

"I could not see anyone, but at Clark, they have this scout and..." he was cut off.

"I've already heard about this God...this man that's a third white, a third Apache, and a third ghost. I don't want to hear anymore about this man. If you Mexicans are afraid...GET THE HELL OUT," he shouted.

Juan put his hands on the pommel of his saddle and leaning forward said,

"Senor, we are not afraid, just cautious. This man is not to be taken lightly. That is all we meant."

"There's a spring about a half mile north...why don't we go there and rest up." Santos said. They headed toward the spring. No one paid any attention to Yancey glancing over his shoulder...looking... wondering.

~~~

The patrol was several miles from Clark. Tye, in front about a quarter mile, had just found where the gang had left the Old Mail Road and headed northwest. He stopped, waiting for the patrol to reach him. He was pleased with the men O'Malley had picked. They, along with Garrison, Corporal Arnold, and Sergeant Rankin, made up in experience for what they lacked in numbers. He had been in fights with bandits and Apaches with each of them and every one of them has 'the hair of the bear' as his pa used to say of mountain men that were hell on wheels in a fight. He had a feeling before this patrol was over, every one of them would be tested.
~~~

"They headed northwest, Lieutenant," Tye said when the patrol arrived.

"How far behind are we?"

Tye dismounted, found a good track in a sandy area where it wasn't hard packed dirt and rocks and traced it with his finger, checking how much it had filled in. He stood up, looked to the northwest, where the tracks headed.

"Figure one, no more than two hours. They've slowed down to a walk... figure no one's following them."

"Then we should be able to make up some ground on them." Garrison said taking off his hat and slapping it on his thigh to get the dust off. "Let's ride." Tye reached over and grabbed the Lieutenant's horse's bridle.

"Hold on a minute, Lieutenant. We've pushed our mounts pretty hard. One thing I've learned living out here, don't push your mounts too hard when it's not neccessary. You may need them fresh at any time...could save your life some time. My suggestion would be to take about a thirty minute break...water and feed the horses and give the men a break." Garrison thought about it a minute, then turned to his men.

"Thirty minutes...take care of your mounts."

After watering and feeding Sandy, Tye was giving him a good brushing. They had taken to each other like bisquits and butter. Sandy had saved Tye's hide more than once...once by outrunning a bunch of Apaches and again by alerting him to an ambush. His ears twitching saved Tye's hide that time. Man could learn a lot by watching and knowing his horse's manners his pa used to say. Corporal Arnold walked up.

"What do you think, Tye?" Arnold asked.

"Think about what?"

"The bunch we're after."

Tye put the brush in the saddle bags, rested his arms on the saddle staring off in the distance. "I figure we're going to get damn bloody on this one, Del. Those men ain't likley to give up. They know they will hang, so they will fight. From what the man said that saw them in San Antonio, they're animals and give no thought to killing someone."

"Figured as much. One thing for sure though."

"What's that?"

"The men riding with us are good men. I've been on patrol with each of them many times, shared good times...and rough times. They all got sand and will stand with you."

"I know. Ain't worried about them."

"What's got you worried then?"

"This." Tye pulled a cartridge out of his pocket.

"What's that?"

"A 44/40 calibre cartridge."

"So."

Tye walked over to a large rock and sat down. "Fits one of them repeating rifles; probably a Henry. If each of them has one, we're walking into a lot of firepower...a hell of lot more than we have."

"Sweet Jesus. Does Garrison know this?" Del said staring at the cartridge in his hand.

"He's fixing to."

"Know what?" Garrison said walking up to them.

"Tye thinks the men we're after have repeating rifles."

"That true, Tye?"

"Show him the cartridge, Del." Del handed Garrison the cartridge. Garrison rolled it around in his hand for a minute.

"Never saw one before. You sure, Tye?"

"Sure as spring follows winter. Just don't know how many rifles they have. Like I told Del, this could get bad in a hurry if we ain't careful. I think the Henry holds thirteen rounds and can be fired about as fast as you can work the lever. While we are firing three maybe four rounds with these Spencers, they are firing thirteen. Gives a man something to think about doesn't it?" Tye smiled, tighten the saddle girth on Sandy, and then mounted. "Let's go."

"MOUNT UP." Garrison hollered.

Tye rode out in front almost a quarter mile. He was following the tracks, keeping a sharp eye on possible ambush sites at the same time. It bothered him some that the men they were after were taking their merry old time. Why did they not head into Mexico? Why northwest where there is nothing but deep canyons, rocks, cactus, and emptiness except for a few scattered homesteaders? The homesteaders would have nothing they would want. Lots of questions...he needed to come up with some answers...and quick.

~~~

Forty miles or so northwest of where the patrol was, Joshua Freeman surveyed the three quarter's built adobe home and placed his hand on his father's shoulder. "Looks good, pa. All we need is a roof and we can move in and get out of that damn cave." For two weeks they had been living in a large cave on the Rio Grande. The cave's walls were covered by old paintings. They were old...hundreds, maybe thousands of years old. Pa Freeman studied his two son's handiwork.

"Ya'll did right good, son. Yes sir, right good. Let's go in." They walked thru the open door into the living area and kitchen. The room was about twenty by twenty. Two small rooms and two large rooms joined the main room. The large rooms were for Joshua and his wife, Annie, and the other for his brother, Joseph and his wife, Jenny. One of the small rooms was for Joshua's daughter, Sarah and Joseph's daughter, Marcie. Bunk beds had been built for the other room where the four boys would sleep... Joseph's son, Joe Jr. was eighteen and Joshua's sons, Jacob nineteen, Caleb seventeen, and William were fifteen. Pa Freeman would sleep on a pallet by the fireplace. He never like beds...spent too much time trapping, hunting, and wandering.
~~~

The family left their home in Virginia over three months ago. There wasn't much left after the war. Joshua and Joseph both served the Confederacy, fighting under the command of Beauregard at the First Battle of Bull Run and then both were wounded later, at Shiloh. Both boys had always been good with their hands. They bought two old Conestoga wagons and pretty much rebuilt them. When they were through, the wagons were better than when they were new. They loaded what belongings they could and headed west, toward Texas.

They stopped when they came to the junction of the Rio Grande and Pecos Rivers. They spent what money they had buying stock from some Mexicans...twenty chickens and two roosters; three cows and seventy goats to go along with their oxen and horses. They would have their staples; eggs from the chickens, milk from the cows and meat from the goats. They would raise what vegetables they could and gather berries and other edible plants from the land. There was also deer and antelope and an occasional stray buffalo. Things were looking good for them.

~~~

A few miles to the southwest from where the Freemans were, the Cates gang was taking a break. Yancey, Billy, Jake, and Jarrod sat away from the others...the Mexicans. They were one gang okay, but the complete trust wasn't there. Neither knew if it was racial or something else. Yancey was still upset that Juan had spoken to him the way he did...in fact, it stuck in his craw and wouldn't go away. He knew he would have to kill him for it to be gone. Killing someone wasn't new to him; it seemed he had been doing that for as long as he could remember.

Yancy and Billy had ridden with Quantrill during the war...and afterwards. They were part of the most efficient behind the Union lines raiders the Confederacy had during the war. Unfortunately, the raiders became know as cold blooded
~~~

killers. Yancy and Billy were in on the Lawrence, Kansas massacre where they killed two hundred civilians, both men and boys. Among his friends that rode with Quantrill were the James boys, Jesse and Frank, and Cole Younger. They had grown numb to seeing dead men and to killing. He had killed men before for less than what Juan had done.

Jake and Jarrod had ridden together for over a year. They had killed also but were not as callous to it as the Cates were. They would kill if need be but not just for the hell of it. The other four were new to this bandito lifestyle and had been in on a couple of robberies but had not killed anyone, not even in the shindig that just happened in Brackett. All the killing had been done by the Cates, Jarrod, and one of the Mexicans. They were untested and not trusted yet by the Cates.

Santos, who been scouting ahead, rode back into camp.

"Anything up that way?" Billy asked when Santos dismounted and walked into camp.

"Bout three or four miles further the Pecos and Rio Grande run together. There's a homestead being built. Watched for awhile; they don't look like they have much except some livestock and chickens...and some young girls and a couple of women."

"Horses?" Yancey questioned.

"Few, maybe six or seven. Look more like working horses than riding horses."

"Whatcha think Yancey?" Billy asked.

"Let's me and you take a look. You two wanna come?" Yancey questioned Jarrod and Jake. They both nodded and stood up and walked over to their horses. The four rode out. Yancey instructed the six Mexicans to put a man on lookout as he rode out.

When they were out of the camp, Juan walked over to the smoldering coals and picked up the coffee pot.

"They can go to hell. I've had enough of them telling me what to do and when to do it. I'm finishing this cup of coffee and I'm outa here."

"I've done a lot of things I regret," Jesse Valdez said. "This bunch is as bad as they get. They're going to get us all shot or hung. I'm with you, Juan."

The Cortez brothers looked at each other and nodded their agreement as did Lupe Ortiz and Manuel Soto. "There was no excuse for the killing of all those men in Brackett. Can't see us dying being servants to these white men and the way things are now...that's what we are," Lupe said.

They all poured what remaining coffee they had on the coals and then kicked dirt on them to put them out. Throwing their saddles on their horses, they were unaware they were being watched.

~~~

High on a hill maybe a quarter a mile away, Tye was watching the proceedings in the camp thru his binoculars. He saw the four white men ride away earlier. He saw these men looking like they were preparing to leave also. He knew they were part of the gang that he had been trailing but couldn't figure out exactly what was going on. He hurried back down the hill to Garrison and the rest of the patrol.

"They were camped just over the hill but the four white men rode out a few minutes ago and the Mexicans look like they are fixing to leave."

"What do you suggest we do?" questioned Garrison. "Split and go after both?"

"These are cold bloodied killers, Sir. That would be asking for disaster. I think we take what we can first, and that would be the six that are fixing to ride out." The men stood around waiting for Tye to tell them what he thought they should do. "There are only three ways those men can go...south, back the way they come, north the way the others
~~~

went, or east. They can't go west because of the cliff over looking the Rio Grande."

"What way do you think?" Arnold asked.

"Don't know for sure, but from watching their actions I think they had a disagreement and split. I know they have to figure we are tracking them so I don't think they will come back this way nor if they did split, I don't think they will follow the others."

"Its east then," Garrison said.

"I'm fairly familiar with the lay of the land here. We can head down this canyon here and get ahead of them. Maybe surprise them and capture them without getting bloody. Let's ride." Tye said turning Sandy around and heading east, up the canyon.

~~~

It was now late afternoon and the Freemans had decided to eat their evening meal in their new, roofless adobe home. The mood was light and the food was good. Each thought nothing but good times were ahead. Joshua brought out his fiddle and began playing...soon all were singing. The sun was setting and darkness soon would settle around the home. Joshua lit a kerosene lamp and the dim light made shadows dance on the walls as the family moved around the room. Pa Fleming was as happy as the rest, but his years of living in the outdoors would not let him let his guard down completely. He had survived many a fight with Indians and outlaws because he wasn't careless...or stupid.

"SHHHH," he said loudly to the others. "Be quite for a minute."

"What is it, grandpa?" asked Annie. "Did you hear something?"

"Just be quite," he said and walked over to the wall where his rifle was. It was so quite now you could hear one another breathing, almost hear their heart beating. Then they
~~~

all heard it...horses...and they were close...real close. Joshua and Joseph grabbed their rifles as did Joshua's oldest son, Jacob.

"Is it Indians?" a terrified Macie cried.

"It ain't injuns," grandpa said. "Those are shod horses."

"HELLO THE HOUSE." Things were quite in the adobe. No one said anything. Once again the voice rang out.

"HELLO THE HOUSE!" Grandpa and Joshua looked at each other for a second.

"What do you want?" Joshua asked.

"Just a little food and coffee. Been riding a long time. We smelled your food and coffee a mile back yonder." Billy smiled. Old Yance was pouring on the charm. "Sure did smell good...sorta got our bellys growling."

"You boys just get on down the trail. We got no food to spare." Grandpa replied.

"Well now, that ain't very neighborly of ya'll."

"Reason I'm as old as I am...don't take no chances," Grandpa answered sharply. "NOW GIT!" They could hear the men talking, but their voices were too low to make out what was being said.

"What do you think, Grandpa?" Joshua whispered.

"They're up to no good...I promise you that."

"How do you know?"

"My gut son. Got a feeling in my gut...always trusted it before...it's usually right." Suddenly, they heard the sound of hoofs striking rocks moving away from the house.

"Whatcha think now, pa?" Jacob asked, his shaky voice betraying his nervousness. Joshua looked at grandpa.

"They'll be back." Grandpa said.

~~~

The patrol had ridden hard and Tye felt they were well ahead of the six men he had seen leave the camp. He was
~~~

looking for a place they could trap them and give them a chance to give themselves up. The terrain here was condusive to an ambush but it would not be a killing ambush...not at first anyway. Tye found what he thought was a perfect spot. The canyon narrowed to less than fifty yards, huge boulders on the sloping walls for his men to hide behind, and not much protection on the canyon floor for the bandits. He had the men cut some mesquite and go back up the trail they had come in and drag the branches behind their horses wiping out most of the tracks. When they returned, he positioned each man. He would halt the riders and see if they would give up.

Everyone was in position...waiting. They didn't have to wait long...maybe ten minutes before they heard the horses. Arnold was low on the right side of the canyon and Garrison was on the left. If the men jumped their horses and tried to run through the end of the canyon, they were to stop them. The others were on each side of the canyon. All had orders from Garrison not to fire till Tye did. Tye was on Sandy, in the middle of the canyon, just around a bend. The bandits would not see him till they were within ten yards of him. Tye was hoping the surprise would give him and the others an edge.

The riders were close to the bend. Each of the troopers, hidden in the rocks, were ready. Sweat trickled down their faces even though the weather was pleasantly cool and each was lost in their own thoughts and fears. Typical reactions even from seasoned veterans going into a fight when there was the possibility men were going to die. Tye sat on Sandy and had him standing at an angle. His right side was away from where the outlaws would be; the gun in his right hand, invisible to them. He shifted his butt in the saddle and kicked his feet out of the stirrups. If things went bad, he would fire one quick shot, and hit the ground rolling. The bandits were seconds from coming around the bend in front of Tye. Tye took a quick glance at Garrison and then at Arnold and saw they were ready.

The riders appeared around the bend just as Tye looked back. The two lead riders jerked their horses to a stop and the others bumped into them. The surprise was plain on their faces but they quickly recovered. The man in front put his hands on the pommel of his horse. He looked around for others, but saw none. Turning back to Tye, he asked.

"Gringo, what are you doing here?"

"Looking for you."

"Me; why you look for me?"

"Think you and your compadres killed some men in Brackett."

Juan pointed to his chest and looked at the other men with him.

"We killed no one, Gringo. Now move aside." Tye didn't flinch.

"Gotta take you back. If you weren't involved in the shooting, you can go free." Juan and the others laughed heartily.

"You funny, Gringo. There are six of us...one of you. How you gonna do this thing?" Tye just sat there. Juan losing his patience with this white man had more to say.

"Before we kill you, what is your name?"

"Tye Watkins."

The name brought an immediate reaction. Each of the men reached for their guns. Tye brought his gun around and fired point blank range into Juan's chest. Juan cart wheeled backwards off his horse, dead before he hit the ground. All hell broke loose.

Tye did not see Juan's cartwheel as he leaped off Sandy as soon as he fired. He hit the ground rolling with bullets hitting all around him. The other men with Tye opened up. Two bandits were knocked off their horses. The others were firing at the soldiers. Pvt. Davis was hit in the face, the bullet exploding out the back of his head. He tumbled down the slope stopping almost at the bandits' horse's hooves. Tye came up on one knee and knocked another one off his horse.

The remaining riders, Lupe and Juan's brother, Alfonso, made a break for the end of the canyon. Garrison and Arnold knocked them off the mounts with well placed shots.

When the dust settled, the men stood up and looked around. The fight did not last thirty seconds but several men were dead.

"Everyone okay?" Tye asked.

"Davis is down," hollered Pvt. Rivera.

"Mankins' hit," Sergeant Rankin said.

The men came down carefully; watching the Mexicans, making sure some of them wasn't playing dead. Tye went over to Mankins. The wound was bad but probably not fatal...unless infection set in. The bullet entered just above the hip bone and exited low in the back. One look was all it took to see Davis was dead.

"This one is still breathing," Arnold said rolling the Mexican over on his back with his foot. Tye wasn't pleased with the way things worked out. With one dead and one wounded, it would require a third trooper to take them back. Tye wasn't concerned about the wounded Mexican. He wasn't going to live long with a bullet buried near his heart. He walked over to Lieutenant Garrison.

"We're going to have to send a man back with Davis and Mankins." Garrison said.

"Yeah. You need to pick someone quick so we can get after the others."

Garrison turned toward the others. "Private Dancer."

"Yes sir."

“I want you to take Davis's body and Mankins back to the fort. You can find it can't you?"

"Yes sir."

"We'll make a travois for Mankins. I'll give you a dispatch for Major Thurston." Tye had walked off to get the material for a travois. It only took him a few minutes to rig one up and Dancer was on his way with the dead trooper, the wounded Mankins, and the dispatch.

"We have about a hour of daylight left, Lieutenant. Let's get after the Cates."

Chapter Six

Yancey and Billy stood in front of the Freeman's adobe home. Jake and Jarrod were on each side about thirty yards from the open windows. From inside the home they could hear the Freeman's singing various songs from the popular Red River Valley and The Yellow Rose of Texas, to the old stand by religious song, Rock of Ages. Yancey had already decided that the old man was going to die and anyone else that stood in his way of getting the family's money. The family was singing Rock of Ages when Yancey fired his pistol thru the open door. The other three opened up also. Bullets were thick as bees in a hive inside the home but grandpa had been ready for that. Even thought they were singing, everyone was against the walls and not in line with the door or windows. So far, the only damage was to the inside walls where chunks of adobe were being knocked into the air from the bullets.

Marcie was screaming, covering her ears to shut out the nosie of the guns. Sarah was holding tight to her mother, Annie. So far, no shots were being returned by the besieged family. The men were waiting on grandpa's signal before they moved to the windows to fire.

"MY GOD!" grandpa screamed. "MOVE ANNIE!" He saw the kerosene lamp slowly arching thru the air before it crashed into the back wall where Annie and Sarah were huddled. Liquid fire went everywhere, lighting up the interior of the home. Annie had pushed Sarah to the side right before the lamp hit above her. Her clothes were on fire and Joshua rushed to help his wife. Silhouetted against the light of the fire he was an easy target for Yancey and Billy. Two bullets hit him almost at the same time, knocking him into Annie and both fell into the flames.

"DAMN YOU TO HELL!" grandpa screamed, rising to fire his rifle. His bullet hit Billy in the shoulder spinning him around, then falling to the ground. Jacob fired as did Joseph, their bullets missing their targets. More shots came into the home, one striking Caleb in the back and another hitting Joseph's wife, Jenny, in the shoulder.

Some of the 'want to' went out of Yancey when he saw Billy go down. He hollered at Jake and Jarrod to come running, that Billy had been hit. Grandpa was ready and when Jake was running toward Yancey, he cut him down with a bullet in the chest. Joseph missed Jarrod with his shot. All was quite except for the crackling of the fire and the girls crying. You could smell the burned bodies of Joseph and Annie. Yancey got Billy on his horse and he and Jarrod hightailed it northeast, away from the homestead.

The fire was finally out and the remains of Joseph and Annie were covered with a blanket. Jenny was having her shoulder wound tended to by her husband, Joseph and daughter, Marcie. Caleb was dead and had been covered with a blanket in the far corner of the home. It would be a long night. Sarah was devastated by the deaths of her mother, father, and her brother, Caleb. She was being consoled by her oldest brother, Jacob. The sun would be bringing a new day before long...one that Grandpa Freeman wasn't looking forward to...burying his oldest son, his daughter-in-law, a grandson, and wondering about the future.

~~~

The patrol had made camp just as full dark set in. Tye had back tracked to the outlaws' camp and picked up the trail of the Cates brothers, following it till it was too dark to see. Arriving back at camp he was surprised to see almost
~~~

everyone already in their bedrolls. The only one moving about, besides the sentry, was Garrison. Garrison told him everyone was bushed and was in their bedrolls before they finished eating their jerky and drinking their coffee.

"Any left?" Tye asked as he was taking the saddle off Sandy.

"Maybe a full cup and there's plenty of Jerky," Garrison replied. Tye gave Sandy some water and oats before he sat down by the fire with Garrison. Garrison handed him the cup of coffee and two strips of jerky.

Tye smiled at Garrison. "How's your butt, Lieutenant?"

"It would be nice if we walked or galloped tomorrow," he answered laughing along with Tye, "no trotting." There was a moment of silence before Garrison stood up and said he was turning in. Tye finished his coffee and jerky while thinking about the Cates. He could not figure out why they didn't go into Mexico where the army could not touch them. The only thing he could figure was that they didn't think the army would chase them for robbing civilians. Maybe in the excitement they didn't realize they killed two troopers making it the army's business. Whatever the reason, they were in no hurry. It could also be that they were not worried about a few soldiers that had single shot sharps and they having the repeaters. He lay on his bedroll listening to the woeful howling of a distant coyote and wondered if it was an omen. He drifted off to sleep still wondering.

~~~

It was now an hour before daylight and everyone was drinking coffee and re-living the fight yesterday. When they made camp last night, they had been almost too bushed to eat, and certainly in no mood to talk. They were making up for it now.

"That Mex did a double back flip when my old Sharps lit his candle," Private Christian said laughing. "I saw the look in
~~~

his eyes when he saw me sighting down on him...he knew he was dead meat."

"I still think we should have buried them instead of leaving them like that." Private O'Lear added.

Arnold spoke up. "They were sorry pieces of horse dung. Leaving them for the coyotes and buzzards is what they deserved."

"I heard Tye and the Lieutenant talking about the bodies. Decided they couldn't waste time burying them. Only let the others get farther ahead." Sergeant Rankin said.

"Speaking of Tye, where is he?" Christian asked

"I had last watch," O'Lear said. "He rode out about an hour ago; said he'd be back before daylight."

"Hear a horse now," Arnold said. "Probably Tye."

"Tye's coming in," shouted Rivera who was over by the horses. Tye entered the camp, dismounted and made straight for the coffee pot. No one said anything while he poured his coffee. Tye blew on the coffee in his cup trying to cool it a little. He loved coffee but always hated the first sip...always burned his damn lips. This time was no different.

"Be ready in a second, Lieutenant. Let me have a couple swallows of coffee first."

Garrison nodded and turned to the men. "PREPARE TO MOUNT." Each of the men, except Tye, moved to the side of their mounts placing their left foot in the stirrup. Garrison turned to Tye. "Ready, Tye?"

"Let's go," Tye answered mounting Sandy.

"MOUNT," Garrison commanded. The men mounted as one and then squirmed some, getting their butts comfortable in the damnable McClellan saddle. "BY THE TWOS...YO."

Tye galloped Sandy a couple hundred yards out front and then settled down to a trot. The tracks were plain and no problem to follow. The terrain here was rolling hills but would change in a couple, three miles as they got closer to the river. He figured they were still a couple or so hours behind the men now. From the look of the tracks, the bastards were still in no hurry. The temperature was pleasant and Sandy was a little on the frisky side and Tye was having to hold him back.

"Come on, Sandy, settle down." Tye was patting him on the shoulder as he spoke. Sandy nickered and shook his head bringing a smile to Tye. He would swear that Sandy understood every word he said.

The patrol had been moving at a mile eating pace and Tye figured they were only a mile or so from the junction of the Rio Grand and the Pecos rivers. He stopped, took the makings out and rolled himself a smoke, while waiting on the patrol to catch up. Glancing around, he studied this land he loved. He was remembering his pa, who was killed not far from this spot several years ago while serving with the Rangers. He had died in Tye's arms, telling Tye how much he loved him and his ma and for him to take care of her.

The patrol arrived, Tye swallowed to get the lump out of his throat.

"Suggest we take a short break, Lieutenant. Horses need a rest."

'Horses my ass,' Garrison was thinking. 'This trotting has my insides upside down and my legs are like jelly after holding my butt up off the saddle.'

"DISMOUNT!" He stepped off his horse and with both hands massaged his butt.

"Are we gaining on them?" Garrison asked.

"We're gaining...hour, maybe a little more now," Tye answered. He saw the men taking care of their mounts before themselves. He smiled, gave Sandy some water and a good scratching between the ears and at the same time, his eyes were scanning the hills where they were headed. He didn't think the four men left were aware he was as close as he was to them.

~~~
~~~

Damn bullet has got to come out, Billy." Yancey said looking at the hole in his brother's shoulder. "Ain't gonna quit smarting till it does."

"Make camp and get it out." Billy answered. Yancey turned to Jarrod.

"We're gonna stop long enough to get the lead out of Billy's shoulder. Ride back a ways and see if anyone is following us." Jarrod rode off and Yancey, who had already dismounted, helped his brother off his horse. "Damned old man that shot you is gonna pay for it...the whole damn bunch is gonna pay." He laid Billy down on a patch of grama grass and then busied himself building a fire.

"Ever dug a bullet out of anyone?" Billy asked, his face a mask of pain behind the sweat that was running down it.

"No, but I seen it done enough in the war."

"That don't make me feel too damn good about it."

"Just relax." Yancey said. He opened a bottle of whiskey. "Drink as much of this as you can, while I get the fire going."

Jarrod returned. "Nothing in sight except some damn buzzards, Yance."

"That's exactly what that old man is going to be when I'm through with him...buzzard bait." Yancey replied. He had gotten the fire going and turned to Billy. "You ready?"

"Ready as I ever will be," he replied in a slightly slurred voice.

"Take another good swallow." Billy did and Yancey took the bottle and poured some of the contents on his blade. "This ain't gonna feel good." Billy smiled and gave Yancy the go ahead with a nod of his head. Yancey placed a piece of rawhide between his brother's teeth. "Chomp down on this, Billy. It'll help some."

Yancey wiped the sweat off his forehead with his sleeve and went to work. He slipped the point in the bullet hole and started probing for the piece of lead. Billy's face was red and his cheeks puffed out trying to keep from screaming.

"FOUND IT!" Yancy exclaimed loudly. He poked his finger in the hole and finally got the lead between his finger and the blade. He carefully lifted the lead out. "Got it Billy; I got the damn thing." He placed the bloody lead in Billy's hand and noticed the hand didn't close on it. Looking at Billy's face he saw he had passed out. He was breathing normal. "Probably best he passed out." He placed the blade in the fire, turning it back and forth. He held it there until it was glowing red. He took Billy's kerchief and wiped the blood away, poured some more whiskey on the wound which brought a groan from Billy. He placed the flat side of the glowing blade over the hole and wiped the flesh with it. Billy moaned some more but that was it. The stench of burnt flesh went away quickly and the hole was seared over.

"Let him sleep, Jarrod. He'll be a lot better in a day or so."

"You mean we're gonna stay here?" Questioned Jarrod. "There's gonna be a patrol after us, Yancy. We killed two soldier boys. That damn Watkins is probably with them." Yancy stood up and looked around. He spotted what he was looking for, a hill about a half mile away with steep angled walls.

"Let's get Billy up there," he said pointing toward the hill.

~~~

Tye was checking out the homestead from a distance. He hadn't seen anyone moving about but the place wasn't deserted because he could see some goats off to the left. He started Sandy toward it keeping a sharp watch in all directions...something wasn't as it should be. As he entered the yard he saw the rifle poking out of the window. He did the customary thing,

"HELLO THE HOUSE."

"Who ye be?" a voice asked from inside the house.
~~~

"Watkins...Tye Watkins." There was a few seconds pause.

"From Fort Clark?"

"Yes. I'm scouting for a patrol from there chasing four men wanted for murder." An old man appeared at the door, the rifle pointed at the ground.

"Heard of you; step down and come on in." Tye dismounted and walked to the man holding out his hand. The old man took it in a firm handshake.

"Name's Freeman; been a long time since anyone called me anything but Pa Freeman."

"Pa it is then Mr. Freeman. What happened here?"

"You said you were chasing four men?"

"That's right."

"Well, there is only three now. One's buried over there." Tye looked at the grave off to one side of the yard and noticed three more that was closer to the adobe home. Freeman saw him looking at the other graves.

"My oldest, his wife, and their son. That man and his companions come in here last night and killed 'em. They were looking to kill us all. Guess they got a little more than they figured 'cause they hightailed it after I wounded another one of 'em."

"Sorry about your kin, Mr. Freeman. Those men, they're a bad bunch; killed five people in Brackett." The patrol came into the yard at that time. Garrison dismounted and handed his reins to Arnold. Walking up to the two men, Tye introduced Mr. Freeman to Garrison and then explained what happened.

"My sincere condolences for your loss, Mr. Freeman," Garrison said putting his hand on the old man's shoulder. "What are you going to do now?"

"Gonna finish what we started. Nothing else we can do." Garrison was surprised at the answer.

"You mean you're going to stay?" Pa Freeman nodded his head.

"I could have answered that myself, Lieutenant. People like these are what it takes to make it out here." Tye said. "These men and women have sand. They have to be tough...it's hard enough to make it out here with the heat, cold, too much rain, not enough rain, ground not really suitable for farming, sickness, loneliness...all these things make it tough out here. After all these problems, throw in the threat of Apaches at any second coming after you and your family. Then when you get comfortable, things are maybe a little better than before, damn bandits come by and try to take it away from you. Yeah, it's tough out here and only a few can handle it." Garrison shook his head then turned back to Freeman.

"Anything we can do for you Mr. Freeman?" Garrison asked.

"You can catch those sumbitches...alive if you can, and bring them by here on your way back to the fort."

"Well get'um Mr. Freeman...you can count on that." Tye promised. "You ready, Lieutenant?" Garrison nodded.

"SERGEANT RANKIN."

"YES SIR." Rankin answered running to the lieutenant.

"Get the men mounted. We're heading out." As they left the yard the old man hollered.

"DON"T YOU SOLDIER BOYS FORGET YOUR PROMISE." Tye turned and waved to him. Corporal Arnold rode up beside Tye and Garrison.

"What's he talking about...what promise?

"Wants us to bring those men back by here...alive." Garrison said.

"ALIVE!" an astonished Arnold shouted. "He's got to be kidding. Those bastards ain't gonna give up. They'll be like a she wolf protecting her pups...meaner than hell. They got nothing to lose...onliest thing waiting for them would be a noose. No sir. You ain't bringing those boys in alive."

Tye chuckled. "You got it all figured out there, Arnold."

"Hell, it ain't hard."

"We'll see." Tye said and kicked Sandy in the flanks, moving out ahead of everyone.

"You're serious aren't you, Lieutenant?" Arnold asked. "About bringing those men in?"

"Yes sir."

"If we can. If there's any way."

"They're meaner than a damn rattler, Sir."

Garrison nodded his head toward Tye. "What do you think he is, Corporal...an angel?" Arnold thought about that for a couple seconds. He nodded his head and smiled.

"You may be right. Maybe there's a chance."

~~~

Billy was resting peacefully on top of the hill that Yancey had picked out. He lay in the shade of a large cedar. Yancey was sitting on a rock, watching a rider in the distance. Jarrod had seen him earlier and pointed him out to Yancey.

"It's than damn scout, Watkins...I'd bet my life on it," he commented. The rider, about a half mile away, had dismounted, apparently looking at the ground. He was at the spot where Yancey had removed the bullet from Billy. Jarrod had taken great pains to erase all their tracks with a mesquite limb. "What's he doing?" he asked Yancey who was watching the man thru a pair of binoculars.

"He's got the trail," Yancey said; "Looks like he's looking straight at us."

"It's got to be him."

"Dammit, he'll bleed just like you and me if you put a bullet in his ass. Something special... hell." He spit in disgust.

"Say what you want and think whatever you want. He's not normal...even the damn Apaches fear him." Jarrod said.

"There's the patrol coming up to him." Yancey said, handing the glasses to Jarrod.

~~~

"What do you think, Tye," Garrison asked when he dismounted and walked to Tye who was on one knee, looking off in the distance.

"They did their best to cover their tracks but missed some. Looks like they worked on the injured man. Found this in a bush over there." he pointed to a bush a few yards away and handed the bloody kerchief to Garrison.

"Looks like the old man was right...he winged one of them." Garrison commented.

"They made a travois and took him there," Tye said pointing to the hill that Yancy was on. "Figure they wanted the high ground in case someone was following them." Garrison stood up and looked at the ground...saw nothing that indicated to him that the men were there but he learned awhile back that Tye could read tracks like he could read a book so he didn't question him.

"If they are there, they have the high ground and that's an advantage." He said.

Tye, scratching his chin, said "Maybe so... maybe not."

"What do you mean by that?"

"As far as advantage in a fight, yeah, they do. But I bet they didn't think of one thing."

"What's that?"

"Water... food. They can't have much. They got none at the homestead. I figure they are a little short on both and a wounded man is gonna need more than ususal. I think they got themselves in a bind...they just don't know it yet."

"I know better than to question you...but how can you be sure they are up there?"

Tye laughed. "Saw a reflection awhile ago. They are probably watching us thru binoculars." Garrison chuckled and shook his head.

"Let's get the hill surrounded and get this over with as soon as possible." Tye said while mounting Sandy.

~~~
~~~

"Dammit to hell, Yancey. What have you got us into?" Jarrod was livid. "In a few minutes they will have men all around this damn hill you got us on, and no way out. What the hell were you thinking?"

"Calm down ole boy." Yancey answered smiling.

"CALM DOWN!!!CALM DOWN!!! HOW IN HELL CAN YOU TELL ME TO CALM DOWN YOU STUPID BAST..." He never finished as Yancey slapped him hard across the face. Jarrod went for his gun but Yancey was quicker and already had his out.

"Jarrod, listen to me. I should have told you before but that's water under the bridge now. We, that is, Billy and me, were meeting some friends of ours near here. There are about twenty of them...all experienced fighting men. They will get us out of here."

"When?" A more relaxed Jarrod asked.

"Sometime tonight or early tomorrow. We'll just have to hold tight till then. I think the soldier boys will expect to starve us out and won't risk any men by coming up here. Remember your lessons in warfare...always try and have the high ground."

Jarrod looked hard at his friend. "You didn't feel me and ole Jake deserved to be in on your plans. We've been thru a hell of a lot together for you not to trust us."

"I know that. I just wish Jake was alive so I could apologize to him also. Don't know what I was thinking." Yancey said in a very uncharacristic apologic tone. "Should have let ya'll in on the plan."

"In on what plan?"

"Billy, me, and you along with the meanest bunch of men you ever saw are going to sweep across this land along the border raiding ever home we come to. Gonna make Apaches look like saints with what we're gonna do." He stuck out his hand, offering it to Jarrod. "Hope you accept my apology." Jarrod shook his hand and Yancy tightened his grip and jerked Jarrod forward...right into his Bowie he held in his left hand. The blade entered Jarrod's belly just above the navel, buried all the way to the hilt. Yancey twisted it and ripped it upwards, the razor sharp blade gutting Jarrod like one would do a deer. Jarrod never uttered a word, a look of shock on his face, bloody froth coming from his lips. His eyes fixed, and Yancey let him fall to the ground.

"No one calls me a bastard and gets away with it you sonofabitch." He kicked him hard in the ribs and then walked over to where Billy lay. Looking back, he smiled and muttered, "Anyway, now Billy and me have a little more water." He laughed and sat down in the shade of the mesquite beside his brother. Billy was moaning some, starting to come around which Yancey was glad to see.

"Lance and the rest will be here soon, Billy," he said pouring a little water on his kerchief and placing it on Billy's forehead. Lance, and some of the other men, was with Yancey and Billy when they were riding with Quantrill. Lance was like Yancey, tough as nails, meaner than a she bear in a fight, and could be trusted as much as his own kin could be.

Billy opened his eyes.

"Did you get the bullet out?"

"Hell yes...several hours ago," Yancey answered laughing.

"Several hours?"

"That whiskey put you out like a light. Best thing for you, too."

"Where are we?" Billy asked looking around.

"On top of a hill...surrounded by soldiers."

"SURROUNDED?"

"Settle down, Billy. Lance and the boys will be here soon."

Billy lay his head back down and closed his eyes. "Get shot...pass out...wake up...shoulder hurts like hell... now find out I'm surrounded... Damn!" Yancey laughed at his brothers comments.

"At least you still have a sense of humor. Just relax and go back to sleep if you can...help will be here soon."

Chapter Seven

It had been almost three hours since the patrol had the small hill surrounded. With no more men than they had, there were gaps in the perimeter where no one was. The gaps were however not so great they could at least be covered by two guns that could catch anyone trying to escape in crossfire... if they could see them. It was going to be dark shortly, and Tye wasn't comfortable with the situation at all. He was on the south side with Arnold to his left and Private Christian on his right. All the men were at least fifty to seventy five yards apart. Tye knew this was okay during the day but at night, they were vulnerable to having someone slip thru the lines. He was hoping for a windless night so that any noise would be heard. It would be hard to be absolutely quite moving a man and a horse on the rocky ground.

Thirty minutes before dusk, Tye made the rounds making sure each man had water and some jerky to chew on. Each man was told to shoot anything that moved after dark and that they were to stay put...if they had to relieve themselves, do it where they were. Garrison was on the north side with privates O'Leary and Rivera and Sergeant Rankin, privates Molar and Roberts on the east. Tye wasn't worried about the west side; a forty foot vertical drop into an arroyo ran along the entire base of the hill there.

It was dark by the time Tye got back to his post. Making himself comfortable, he settled in for the night...at least that was what he thought. He happened to look over his shoulder and was surprised to see a small fire maybe two or three miles away. 'Who in the hell could that be,' he thought to himself. Looking back up the hill he saw the small fire was now a large one. ‘Only a stupid man, or there were enough men they wasn’t worried, would make a fire that big.’ He thought for a minute then swore outloud. “Damn signal fire." Moving quietly, he walked to where the horses were picketed. He had to see who was at the other fire. Tightening the girth on Sandy, he walked him until he knew he was out of hearing of anyone, mounted, and rode toward the fire.

About two hundred yards from the campfire, he dismounted and continued on foot, his moccasin boots making no noise on the rocky ground. He could hear talking and laughing coming from the men around the fire. Crawling on his belly, he got within thirty feet of some of the men. He could hear them plain now.

"Old Cates should be at the fire on that hill," one said.

"We'll be there at first light," said another, and then added. "Old Yancey has big plans for us boys...big plans."

"What plans, Lance?"

"Don't know for sure but you can bet there's going to be some profit in it and probably some killing."

"What about women?" asked an other.

"Gonna be plenty. All these homesteads have wives and daughters." Lance answered back.

"That's whut I wanted tu heer," a big oaf with a full black beard and a buffalo robe on said, slapping the man's shoulder sitting next to him and laughing heartily.

Tye listened for a couple minutes more, hearing more comments that told him this was one mean bunch and aimed to do a lot of killing along the Border...to people he knew and cared about. Backing out the way he came in, Tye's mind was working, trying to come up with a way to stop them. He knew they were outnumbered two or three to one. His first responsibility was to his men back at the hill. They would be slaughtered in the morning when this many men rode in from behind them. Finding Sandy, he mounted and rode back to the hill.

When he arrived he made no attempt at being quiet. Stopping Sandy, he hollered at Arnold and Christian. "This is Tye, you men come to me." When Arnold and Christian got to him, Tye dismounted. "We have a problem, men. Christian, go get the others and bring them here. Don't be quiet about it. Make sure they know it's you." He left and Tye sat on a large rock.

"What's the problem?" Arnold asked.

"Bout two miles or so yonder where that campfire is,"Tye said pointing, "is twenty or so of the meanest looking bunch of men you ever saw."

"What's that got to do with us?"

They are coming here in the morning to meet up with the Cates." Arnold let out a low whistle.

"And we're between them."

"That's the problem." Tye said.

Turing toward the sound of rattling rocks Arnold muttered, "Here come the others."

"What is going on, Tye?" Garrison questioned.

"All of you men gather round," Tye ordered. "There are twenty or so men about two miles from here." He pointed and all were looking at the fire. "I saw fire a couple hours ago and I left to see who it was. They are here to meet the Cates."

"Meet the Cates!" Garrison exclaimed. "Are you sure?"

"Sure as I'm standing here. I was close enough to hear them talking. It's the meanest, toughest looking bunch I have ever seen. Talking about killing people like me and you would talk about the weather."

Christian spoke up. "What the hell we going to do? There's twenty to twenty-five of them."

"We'll be fighting them and the Cates will be on the high ground shooting at our backs," an excited O'Leary said.

"First thing we're gonna do is calm down and listen to what Tye has to say." Garrison said. "Now keep quiet and listen."

"I've been thinking about what to do ever since I left their camp. See what you think of this plan, Lieutenant." Tye sat on the rock and everyone else took a knee or sat down, all eyes on Tye.

"I'm gonna injun up the hill and try to surprise and over power the men up there. We can then have the high ground and have a surprise for the other men in the morning when they show up. They don't have a clue that we are anywhere around here so they should just ride in unsuspecting.

"You gonna go up there and capture them by yourself?" Arnold asked.

"Unless any of you have these in your saddlebags," Tye said pointing to his moccasins. "I can move a hell of lot quieter than you can in those boots." With that settled, Tye stood up. "I'll signal you when I'm done." With that said, he dissapeared into the night.

"Whatcha think, Lieutenant?" Private Molar asked.

"Every one of us has seen that man do things time and again that we could never do. We'll wait for his signal and then move up the hill. Molar...you, Christian, and Rivera, get the horses."

"YO," came the answer almost in unison from the men.

"Sergeant Rankin."

"Yes sir."

"You will be in charge of the water, so gather up the canteens. The men will drink only when I say."

"Yes sir."

~~~

Rebecca sat on the porch combing her hair, thinking of Tye, wondering where he was and if he was safe. Buff sat on the porch whittling by the light from the kerosine lamp that filtered out the open door.

"You think Tye and the patrol is okay, Buff?"
~~~

"Sho nuff, Becca. Yu kno Tye's gonna keep thos boys outa truble. Don't ya fret nun now. He'll be bac afore ya kno it."

"I know he can take care of himself, Buff. I always worry he might get hurt helping someone else."

"Thar's always a chance uf tha when ya do whut he duz." Buff laughed at a thought he had.

"What's so funny?"

"Jus membered whut tha doc said about Tye and his wunds. Doc dun tol Tye he'd nev'r die cause he don't hav no vital organs. If'n he did, he'd alrady be dead frum all thos wunds he has all over his bodie." Rebecca laughed.

"He's got a few, that's for sure."

"He's jus like his pappy, Becca...wun uf a kind. Don't yu wurry yo're pretty head too much abut him. He's okay." He went back to his whittling and Rebecca stood up and went into the house. She immediately poked her head back out the door.

"Thanks, Buff." Buff nodded, and continued his whittling.

"I'm glad you're here, Buff. I hope you think hard about what Tye said and stay with us." She turned and went back into the house. "Nite, Buff."

"Gudnite Becca." Buff had been thinking about what Tye had said a lot. He thought he might just take them up. It was nice having a roof over your head and someone to talk to.

~~~

Tye was moving silently up the steep slope. He was taking his time, careful where he placed each step on the rocky ground. He had been climbing for twenty minutes when he stopped to catch his breath just a few feet from the rim. He took his rifle and checked the barrel to make sure it didn't get clogged with dirt during the climb. Satisfied, he inched his
~~~

way a little farther up and peered over the rim. He was shocked to see a body less than three feet away.

'Looks like he's been gutted like a damn deer,' Tye thought to himself. He wondered how that happened but nothing was beyond this bunch, not even killing each other. Raising his gaze from the body, he spotted the other two, about twenty yards away. The fire was between him and them. 'Damn stupid of them to do that.' He was thinking. He raised himself to a crouching position and moved on silent feet toward the two, knowing they could not see him until he got to edge of the light of the fire.

They didn't and he could see the surprise on their faces when he shouted, "UP WITH YOUR HANDS!"

"WHAT THE HELL?" Yancey shouted, reaching for his rifle.

"I WOULDN'T TRY IT," Tye shouted. Yancey's hand stopped a few inches from his rifle, freezing there as he decided to try it or not.

"Make up your mind you murdering sonofabitch," Tye said in a voice showing his disgust. Yancey remembering his friends that would be coming decided to wait.

"Stand up," Tye ordered, "and drop your gun belt and kick them and your rifle toward me." Yancey did as he was ordered.

"Now, get the gun from the wounded man and toss it carefully over toward me." With that done, Tye moved closer to the two men. "I figure you to be the Cates brothers?" he said questionally. Neither man said a word. Tye smiled and walked up to the one standing. He switched the rifle to his left hand and at the same time came up with a vicious right that caught Yancey flush on the chin. The blow lifted the surprised man a foot off the ground and deposited him on his back several feet away. He lay there for a couple of seconds before getting up. He looked at Tye with eyes that burned with hate. Tye moved over to the wounded man, looking at his shoulder wound.

"You as stubborn as he is?" The man didn't say anything. Tye placed his foot on the wound and stepped down. A horrible scream came gushing from the man's throat. The other man made a move toward his rifle and Tye swung his rifle to where it was pointed at the man's belly. "JUST TRY IT." Tye threatened. Cates stopped in his tracks.

"Let's try it again. You the Cates brothers?" Silence followed so Tye put more pressure to the wound with his foot resulting in more screams from Billy.

"Okay, you bastard. I'm Yancey and that's Billy you got your damn foot on."

"Yancey and Billy...Cates?"

"Yeah, we're brothers."

"Turn your back to me and put your hands behind your back." Yancey did as he was told and Tye tied his hands securely, then his feet. He bound the wounded man's hands and feet before walking to the rim and hollered at the men to come on up.

"Told you he could do it." Garrison said to Arnold. Arnold and Rankin just laughed as they all started up the slope, leading their horses. Reaching the top, they picketed their horses, unsaddled them, and walked over to Tye who was sitting on a log by the fire.

"Where's the third one?" Garrison asked.

"Over there," Tye answered, pointing to the right of where they were. Arnold walked over, taking a knee to look at the body. "Been gutted like a deer, Lieutenant." Garrison looked at Tye.

"Mr. Cates there killed him...killed his own man; hadn't got around to asking him why."

"Ain't none of your damn business. Ain't none of you damn, yellow bellied, low-life Yankee business," Yancey said with a sneer. Arnold whirled around and hit him flush on the nose with a wicked right. Yancey staggered backwards, his busted nose bleeding all over his shirt.

"You're one tough hombre soldier boy, when you are hitting a man whose hands are tied," Yancey yelled. Arnold spun him around, pulled his Bowie and slashed the bindings on Yancey's hands.

"WHAT ARE YOU DOING?" Garrison yelled at Arnold.

"Gonna teach this sonofabitch something he's never going to forget." He said. "This murdering piece of shit has killed a lot of people in cold blood. He's gonna suffer some now."

Tye stepped in smiling. "Know how you feel, Corporal but you could lose your stripes if you hit a prisoner. Now me on the other hand," Tye turned and hit Yancey on the chin with a tremendous right that lifted the man again off the ground and a full five feet backwards. Yancey was unconscious before he hit the ground.

"Now tie his hands back," Tye said. "He ain't gonna be flapping his lip for awhile."

"What the hell was that all about?" Rivera asked coming in from sentry duty and looking at the unconscious outlaw.

"A lesson." Arnold answered.

"A lesson? What the hell are you talking about...a lesson?"

"Speaking lessons." Sergeant Rankin said laughing.

"Yeah, that's right. Tye was just giving him some speaking lessons." Arnold said laughing with all the rest. Rivera looked at each of them, turned, and walked away looking back over his shoulder, hollered. "Every one of you are crazy." His remarks caused even more laughter, even Tye had to smile

Tye looked up at the night sky, staring at the stars. "Must be about midnight," he muttered. Arnold looked at the stars then took out his pocket watch. It was ten minutes after. He showed the watch to Rankin. They both looked up at the stars, then each other, shaking their heads. Arnold had to ask.

"Tye, tell us something. How in hell, with all that's gone on tonight, did you know the time?"

"When I was a youngster, pa and me spent more nights under the stars than under our roof. Night after night, we would go over the different constellations...their positions at certain times of the year and even at certain times of the night. By using the pointers of the Big Dipper, knowing what time they are pointing in a certain direction tells you the time. Pretty simple once you get the hang of it. People been doing it for countless years. Ain't exactly accurate to the minute but I can usually get within less than half hour...close enough usually."

"Is there any damn thing your pa didn't teach you?" Rankin asked.

"How to control my temper," Tye replied laughing and walking away.

"Lieutenant, what are we going to do in the morning when that bunch rides in?" Rankin asked.

"I'm not sure yet. I'll speak with Tye in a few minutes about it and we'll come up with a plan. Whatever we decide, we have the element of surprise on our side. Arnold, you relieve Roberts in a couple hours then Christian you relieve Arnold for the last watch. Now, you men get some sleep." He left to go speak with Tye.

"Get some sleep he says," Christian said. "How in hell does he expect a man to go to sleep when he knows he's gonna be in a fight at first light and he's outnumbered at least three to one?"

"One thing's for sure, private, you can't be killed but once," Arnold said snickering. "Now shut up so a man can get his rest." Christian thought that was about the stupidest remark he had ever heard. He pulled his blanket up to his chin and looked at the black sky with its thousand twinkling stars; trying to put everything out of his mind... it wasn't working.

Chapter Eight

Garrison slept only a couple hours and getting out of his bedroll blew on his hands to warm them as he walked up to where Tye was brushing Sandy. "Chilly tonight."

"That time of the year, Lieutenant." Tye said. "Couldn't sleep, Lieutenant so I've been doing some hard thinking; being outnumbered the way we are, I think the best thing to do is take the fight to them."

"You mean...attack?"

"They aren't aware of us being here and from watching them, they aren't organized enough to have sentries. We hit them at first light, we might get lucky and get them to thinking there are more of us than there are."

"You actually think they might?" Garrison questioned.

"Not really," Tye laughed, "but it was a interesting thought. They're hard cases, Lieutenant...like none I've seen before. But if we hit them from behind the rocks and trees, we have a chance. Their camp is pretty much in the open. Like I said, they aren't expecting trouble."

"If you think that's the best way...then that's the way it will be." Garrison said getting up. "When do we leave?"

"Two hours before daylight."

"I'll have the men ready."

~~~

Back at the fort, Rebecca, wrapped in a shawl, had come back out on the porch. It was well past mid-night, but she had not been able to go to sleep. A board had squeaked
~~~

slightly as she walked softly across the room to the door. Buff, alert even while sleeping from years of surviving outdoors, woke immediately. He slipped his pants over his longjohns quickly, picked up his rifle and quietly opened the door of his room. Seeing no one, but noticing the front door open, he moved quickly and silently to it and looked out.

"Whatcha doing out heer?" he asked. Rebecca almost jumped out of her skin when he spoke.

"Buff, you startled me."

"What's the matter, Rebecca?"

"Couldn't sleep, Buff; I think Tye's in trouble... or fixing to be." Buff scratched the back of his neck.

"Whut makes yu think tha?"

"I don't know. I just woke up and had this strange feeling. I can't say what it is, just a feeling that something is wrong." Buff propped his rifle against the wall and walked over to her. He took her hand. "Let's sit on tha porch an talk it out." They sit down and2 Buff looked up at the sky.

"Wal, this heer ain't Kolorado but tha ski is jus as purty heer as thar," he said. Rebecca looked up and then put her head on his shoulder. Buff was surprised and didn't know what to do, so he just sat there, not moving. "I love him so much, Buff. I didn't think that it was possible to care for someone like I do Tye."

"I ain't knowed yu and Tye fur long but wun thang I do kno fur sur, that man of yurs luves ya as much as yu luve him. A blind man culd see that. Nev'r seed two peeple as much in luve as yu two. Truth be knowed, I'm sorta jelous. Nev'r had no wun luve me like that."

Rebecca raised her head and kissed him on the cheek. His smell reminded her of her father. "That's a nice thing to say, Buff."

"Jus sayin whut I have seed. Yu two sur make no seckrat abut yur feelins fur eech uther."

"That obvious, huh?" she asked.

"Like to luv birds." answered Buff laughing.

"His pa got himself killed, Buff. I don't know what I would do if something happened to him." There was silence for a moment as Buff was trying to figure what to say.

"I kno'd Ben got himself kilt, Rebecca, but he liv'd manee a yeer and had manee a damn fites befo he did. I kan onlee promise yu wun thang, that thar yung whippersnapper is too onree to be kilt. He's fine, Rebecca. He's fine now and will be tumorrow, yu kan count on that." Rebecca hugged his neck.

"Thanks again, Buff." She stood up. "I feel much better."

"That's gud to kno, Rebecca. Now, yu go ahead an go ta bed. I'm gonna sit out heer fur awhile."

"Thanks again, Buff. I'll see you in the morning."

"Rebecca," he said as he sat back down on the steps, "Didn't we hav this heer Konversation befor?"

Rebecca laughed, "Yes, we did. I just needed to be reasurred again."

Buff took out his pipe, filled it and lite it. He took in some of the sweet tobacco smoke, held it for a minute, and then blew a perfect ring of smoke, the ring suspending in the still night air for a moment before disappearing. He leaned back against the post supporting the roof over the porch and relaxed. 'Buff,' he thought to himself, 'you are home. For the first time in your sorry life, someone cares for you...and you for them. Tye said it was up to me to decide about staying here or not.' Tears welled up in his eyes. "This is home," he said out loud. He sat there smoking his pipe for a few more minutes then stood up, emptied his pipe, and went inside to go back to bed. He slipped his pants back off and sat on the edge of the bed. He felt good...real good.

~~~

Tye shook Garrison's shoulder to wake him up. "Time to get started, Sir." Garrison sat up, scratched the back of his
~~~

neck and stood up. Tye had the rest of the men stirring around, getting their bedrolls and gear ready to ride.

"Check your weapons." Garrison ordered, then looked at Tye and smiled. On previous patrols Tye was always harping about the men keeping their weapons clean and useable. Tye had to smile back.

"Maybe some of my talking has rubbed off after all, Lieutenant."

"Just figured I'd say it before you did. I know how you are about clean weapons." Sergeant Rankin walked up to them.

"Horses are saddled and ready, Sir."

"Good, we leave in five minutes," Garrison said.

"Yes sir."

Exactly five minutes later the command was given to mount up and the patrol was moving out. The importance of being quite had been impressed on each man by both Garrison and Tye. They would dismount three hundred yards from the camp of the outlaws and move into position on foot. Garrison had explained the plan he and Tye discussed while the men cleaned their weapons. Tye would position each man, spaced out so they would surround the camp. They would fire their rifle then use their pistols. Tye was hoping with so many shots being fired from positions all around the camp, the outlaws would think their numbers were greater than they were and surrender.

With every one in position, it was now a waiting game... waiting until it was light enough to be accurate. This was the toughest part of any fight...the waiting. It was almost a relief when the actual fighting started. Every man has their own thoughts at times like this. Three of the men were married, Tye, Sergeant Rankin, and Private Christian. Tye was no different than the other two. His thoughts were about Rebecca, thankful that Buff was there. Christian's thoughts were of his wife, Linda, who was in San Antonio with her parents. There was no place for a private to bring his family at Clark. He took the good luck charm she had given him a month ago when he last saw her, kissed it, and taking off his hat, placed it inside the lining. Rankin's wife, Lucy, would be up now. She was always an early riser and she would be doing things to keep her mind off the danger her husband faced on these patrols. He said a prayer under his breath asking the Lord to protect him but if things went bad, asked him to take care of Lucy and their daughter, Katy. His eyes misted over at the thought of never seeing them again.

Gray streaks were appearing in the eastern sky and each man was getting set to shoot...shoot to kill. There was still no movement in the camp when Garrison hollered.

"HELLO THE CAMP." He waited for a response, but none came. He took out his pistol and fired it in the air. Blankets flew off the men and all were scrambling for the weapons. They thought they were being attacked and a couple of the men fired their weapons. All hell was turned loose by the troopers as a deadly rain of lead shredded the camp. Men were screaming, guns were firing, men were being struck by bullets...complete chaos was in the camp. The chaos only lasted for a few seconds though as the camp become organized quickly and a defensive perimeter as set up. Garrison and Tye both knew immediately that these were ex-soldiers.

Several of the men in camp were down, the rest were returning accurate and deadly fire. Tye saw Roberts get hit and had not re-appeared. He didn't know if he was dead or not. Tye was not aware of it, but Rivera was down also, having taken a bullet that entered his chest and exploded out his back. Things quieted down and it was now a stalemate...both parties were keeping their heads down.

"WHO ARE YOU?" came a voice from the camp.

"Lieutenant Garrison from Fort Clark."

"Why did you attack us?"

"Wasn't going to; didn't know who you were." Garrison lied...but not really. He didn't know who they really were. "You fired on us first."

"That's a damn Yankee lie. You fired first."

"We hollered first but got no response so I fired a shot in the air." Garrison answered. "Who are you?"

"None of your damn business, you stinking blue belly."

"We have you surrounded. I suggest you drop your guns?" Garrison suggested. Tye groaned at the remark. There was a moment of silence before the man answered.

"You're right, you have us surrounded but there's one problem."

"What's that?"

"We counted the smoke. I don't think you have very many men, Lieutenant." At that, they all jumped up and made a run for their horses.

"Dammitt to hell!" Tye hollered, rising up to fire.

Sergeant Rankin and Corporal Arnold were between the charging men and their horses. O'Leary and Molar were on the right and left of the charging men. A murderous fire from the running men riddled Rankin's body and Arnold, firing his pistol as fast as he could, knocked down one man and wounded another before he was hit and went down. Tye brought two of the men down and he saw another stumble and fall, probably the one Arnold had hit. He saw Molar fall and could not see where O'Leary was. Garrison knocked one off his horse as the men rode hard, laying low in the saddle trying to escape the fire from the soldiers. Tye ran to the down men as did Garrison. He ran by the obviously dead Rankin to where Arnold was.

Kneeling down, he turned Arnold over and was relieved he was alive. He was hit hard, one in the side and one in the leg, just above the knee. It appeared the one in his side went clean thru and the one above the knee missed the large bone. Tye was thankful his friend was alive and the wounds was not life threatening. He was in some serious pain though. Tye picked him up and laid him down on one of the outlaw's blankets.

"Ran out of damn bullets," Arnold said grimacing.

"You knocked one down and probably hit another Del. You did great standing your ground like that."

"Too damn scared to run, Tye."

"I'll tell you one thing, Del. You can ride with me any time you damn well please." He shook Del's hand. "Take care of yourself."

"You watch out yourself, Tye. That's one mean bunch and you know they will be coming."

"Figure you're right about that." Tye turned and walked to where Garrison, Christian, and Roberts were. Garrison had a wrap around Roberts' head. He had a scalp wound that had left him unconscious for a few seconds.

"You okay, Roberts?" Tye asked.

"Yeah. Got one hell of a headache though."

"Where's the others?" Tye asked referring to O'Leary and Molar.

"Both dead." Garrison replied.

"Damnation." Tye muttered. "How many made their horses?"

"Bout nine or so." Christian answered.

"Counted eight." Garrsion said.

"Maybe eight made it to the horses but two of them are carrying lead." Roberts added.

"You sure, Roberts?" Tye asked.

"Yeah, I'm sure. I was out for a few seconds but when I came around I saw them riding away, two hanging on to the pommels of their saddle."

"You sure?" Questioned Tye again, knowing Roberts had been burned on the scalp and might not have been fully alert. It would help their situation some if they had.

"Hell yes. Before I got hit I saw both get hit in the upper body, probably shoulder."

"Good," Tye said, “that helps some." He turned to Garrison. "Lieutenant, we need to get after them quickly but we need to get Arnold back to the Fort as well as Rankin’s, Molar’s, and O’Leary’s bodies. See if you can make Arnold comfortable and stop the bleeding. I'm going back to get the Cates. See you in about thirty minutes."

Back at the top of the hill, Tye found both Cates still tied...mad and cussing.

"Heard the shooting...was hoping you got your ass shot off." Yancey said wistfully.

"Didn't and ain't going to either. I'm gonna be around when they stretch your damn murdering neck...and your brother's."

"Well now, we'll just have to see about that, Yank. Did you kill all the friends of mine?"

"We hurt them pretty good," Tye answered. Yancey laughed heartily.

"What's so funny?" Tye asked.

"You don't have a snowball's chance in hell of getting me back. Those boys left will hound you every step of the way." He laughed some more...even Billy was laughing.

"Both of you laugh all you want. You're going back to the fort and wait for a hanging. Yancey, I'll make you a promise. If I'm hit, the last thing I will do with my last breath is blow both your damn heads off." The laughing stopped.

Arriving back at the camp Tye found everything ready to move out. The bodies were wrapped in a blanket lying across the saddle of their horses. Arnold was stretched out on a travois behind his horse.

"Who is taking them back to the fort?" Tye asked Garrison.

"Roberts. He knows the way." Garrison answered. Tye walked over to Roberts.

"When you get back, you look up Mrs. Rankin. You tell her how sorry I am. Her husband was a damn good soldier."

"Roberts, take this dispatch to Thurston," Garrison said as he handed it to Roberts.

"Yes Sir. Anything else, Sir?"

"No, just keep moving and watch for trouble. You sure you can find the fort?"

"No trouble, Sir."

"Move out then."

Chapter Nine

Roberts left for the fort and Tye, Garrison, and Christian, sitting on their horses had to make some quick decisions. They were three and the men they chased totaled eight...maybe six depending on the condition of the two Roberts said were hit. Eight or six, they were all vicious killers, dangerous, and they were mad. On top of that problem, they had Yancey to keep an eye on. They could not send him and Billy back with Roberts. There was no way Roberts could get three bodies, a wounded Arnold and Billy Cates back to the fort while keeping Yancey from killing him if he got the chance.

"Lieutenant, this is the only logical plan I can come up with considering everything." Tye said.

"You're ahead of me then if you have any idea what we can do...I sure don't."

"We can eliminate one problem easy enough."

"I can think of several...which problem you talking about?"

"Yancey. Let's drop him off at the Freemans and let them watch him. It won't be that far off the direction the men are headed."

THE FREEMANS!" Garrison shouted. "MY God, they will kill him as soon as we are out of sight, Tye."

"You have a lot to learn about the people out here, Sir. Sure, I know they have every reason to kill him...but they won't. I only was around them for a short time but I know they are good people, good God fearing people that won't take the law into their own hands."

"You positive, Tye?"

"As sure as anything I have ever been sure of before."

"It would solve one problem for us, that's for sure." Garrison said. "Let's talk to them." Tye jerked Yancey roughly to his feet.

"I'm gonna enjoy killing you, you Yankee bastard." Yancey mumbled. "I'm gonna kill you slow...real slow."

"You ain't the first to think that, Yancey. As you can see, I'm still here." He pushed Yancey from behind toward the horses. Yancey stumbled and almost fell down, mumbled some more cuss words. Tye helped him on to his horse, tying his hands to the pommel of the saddle. He looked back and saw Garrison and Christian were mounted and ready to go. Christian had the reins from Billy's horse, leading him. He noticed the bugle for the first time tied to Christians's pommel of his saddle. "Where did that come from?" Tye asked pointing to the bugle.

"Took it off Molar after he was killed. He loved that ole bugle. It was about the only thing he had besides the clothes he wore. Thought I would take it to his parents one day."

"You know where they are?" Garrison asked.

"Not exactly but he talked about his home enough that I can get close and find them. He was from just north of San Antonio a few miles. They had a homestead there." Tye mounted Sandy, and they were off, headed to the Freemans.

~~~

Two hours later, they entered the yard of the Freeman's.

"HELLO THE HOUSE," shouted Garrison. Not a sound came from the partially built adobe house. For the first time, Tye noticed the tracks of several horses...recent tracks.

"DAMN," Tye cursed as he dismounted, pulled his pistol and made his way to the house. He knew what he was going to find before he ever walked thru the open door. He
~~~

stepped in and took a quick look around...and suddenly felt sick. Lying in the middle of the main room was Pa Freeman, hands tied behind his back, his body riddled with bullets. In one bed room he found the older of the sons, his hands tied behind his back and shot several times. The nude body of his wife was sprawled on the bare floor. He was sure she had been raped several times. She was killed with a bullet in the forehead.

"OH MY GOD," Garrison cried as he entered the house.

"Back here Lieutenant." Tye hollered as he threw a blanket over the woman. He could not remember their names and was upset with that. 'Ain't right to be buried and no name on the head stone except the last name,' he thought to himself. Garrison walked in and saw the two bodies. Tye looked up and thought that Garrison was going to be sick.

"You okay, Lieutenant?"

"How can a man be okay after seeing this," he said sitting down in a chair.

"There's another son and a couple of teenage girls that are missing, Lieutenant." Garrison looked up.

"God! You're right. I forgot about them." he answered.

"Check the other room...okay?" Tye asked as he laid a blanket over the man's body. He heard Garrison curse from the other room. Tye entered the other room where Garrison was covering two girls' bodies with a blanket. The boy's body was sitting against the far wall. If it wasn't for the bullet holes and all the blood, one would think he was just sitting there, staring at the opposite wall. Tye felt it coming...the disgust and anger at this atrocity...the needless waste of human life. As he and Garrison left the homestead, Yancey hollered.

"Hey, Yank, that's just the beginning of the killing." He cut loose with raucous laughter. Tye's disgust boiled over. He ran to Yancey with his Bowie out, slashed the bindings on his hands and jerked him off the horse. He hit heavily on his back with Tye jumping on top of him. Tye's fist was like hammers as he pounded the outlaw's face with rights and lefts. He didn't know how many times he hit him before Christian and Garrison pulled him off the unconscious man...but it was several. His knuckles were bleeding and Yancey's handsome face wasn't so pretty any more. Tye walked over to Sandy, mounted and rode off, following the tracks. He was embarrassed that he had lost control of himself. That wasn't like him and he didn't want to offer explanations right now.

"He going to be okay, private?" Garrison asked looking at the unconscious man.

"Yes sir," Christian answered. "Gonna be pretty damn ugly for awhile. Think his jaw is broke and he has one eye closed." Christian laughed at a thought he had.

"What's so damn funny?"

"Bet this Reb will think twice about opening his filthy mouth around Tye for awhile."

"I won't argue with you about that." Garrison said chuckling. He couldn't believe he was laughing. He just witnessed a man almost beat to death. 'The bastard deserved what he got though,' he thought to himself. They wrapped blankets around the bodies and tied the ends securely. This would have to do until a burial detail could be dispatched from the fort. They could not waste time burying them now because the killers were getting further and further away.

"Let's get this sorry piece of dung on his horse and get after Tye." Garrison said as he helped Christian put Yancey on his horse.

"I know he's out cold, Christian, but make sure he's tied securely to the pommel."

"Yes sir." Christian replied. "Don't worry none about that, Lieutenant. This piece of trash ain't going no where except where we go." He mounted his horse, bent down and picked up Yancey's horse's reins, then looked at Yancey's face.

'That's one feller that's gonna be hurting when he wakes up,' he thought to himself. He smiled, 'deserves every damn thing he got too.'

Tye was waiting for them about a mile from the homestead. When they arrived, he didn't say anything, just turned Sandy, headed south, following the tracks. Garrison was surprised that Tye didn't speak. He looked at Christian and the trooper just shrugged his shoulders. Garrison thought about it for a moment though and figured Tye was a little embarrassed at losing his cool. He had known Tye for six months, been on three long patrols with him, and never seen him out of control. Sergeant O'Malley has known him for almost two years and swears that the man is always in control of himself and whatever situation he was in. The past few hours had brought out another side of Tye...a darker side, and one that Garrison didn't particularly care for. He thought about that for awhile and finally came to a conclusion...one that made him feel better.

"What's with Tye, Lieutenant?" Christian asked. Garrison looked at him for a few seconds saying nothing. "You know, Sir... why isn't he talking to us? Riding off like that without even a 'howdy doo,' is not like him."

"Been thinking about that," Garrison answered. He placed his hands on the pommel of the saddle and raised his butt off the saddle for a couple of moments...it felt good. "Tye is the best there is at what he does...everyone knows that. He's got that way through a hell of lot of hard work and a lot of heartache. He's been learning tracking, fighting and surviving since he was old enough to walk...being taught everything by his pa. He's watched his pa die in his arms and watched his mother die a slow death with a disease no one could figure out. He has watched good friends die at the hands of the Apache and the bandits. He has risked his neck many times saving mine, yours, and every other man at the fort's butts more than once. He has been shot, stabbed, had a couple arrows in him, and has been bashed over the head a few times. He has high standards for himself and for others. He has killed no telling how many Apaches and bandits over the last fourteen years, but not one that was not trying to kill him. He respects the law and despises those who break it. He knows that without some sort of law out here, it would be dog eat dog and most of the time, and the little guy comes out on the short end of the stick. He has strong feelings on what is right and wrong and Yancey represents all that is wrong out here and he just lost it. I'd bet it probably will never happen again... if I was a betting man. In fact, Christian, I don't recall him losing it at all...do you?" Christian looked questionably at him then figured out what the Lieutenant was saying.

"No Sir. I didn't see nothing, except Yancey falling off his horse into some rocks and getting himself all busted up like that." He laughed and Garrison had to smile. He liked this private and figured it was time for him to be promoted. He would speak with Thurston about it when he returned to the fort.

~~~

Lance and his men had stopped on top of a hill to rest their mounts. Looking back the way they had come, they could see no one following them. They had been resting their horses for several minutes and talking about what they did at the homestead. A small amount of money, some grub and whiskey, had been taken plus the satisfaction of killing seven or eight people.

"I'll say one thing for that old man back there," commented Dale, "he was one tough hombre. Most men would have been hollering for mercy after being shot in both knees and shoulders. I almost laughed when he spit in old Curley's face."

"He knew what he was doing," said Curley. "Knowed I'd kill him quick for that."
~~~

"You sure as hell did that," said Lance laughing. "Shot the old bastard right between the eyeballs."

"Shore was some fine women," Curley said. "Sorter hated killing them young ones."

"Hell, Curley, you wouldn't know bad from fine 'cause you ain't ever been particular in your whole sorry life," said Dale laughing.

"And sure as hell never been sorry for killing any one," Curley added.

There were eight men left out of the original twenty. Two of the men, Vince and Steve, were out of action for the time being and in a hell of lot of pain from shoulder wounds.

"What's the plan now, Lance?" Dale asked.

"Going to find what's left of those soldier boys and find out what happened to Yancey and Billy."

"What about Vince and Steve?" Curley asked. "They're hurting pretty bad."

"They'll just have to stay up with us. Their hard luck they went and got themselves shot. Let's mount up and find what's left of those soldier boys."

Chapter Ten

"What did you put in the dispatch to Thurston you sent with Roberts?" Tye asked Garrison as they filled their canteens from a spring Tye knew about.

"That we had Yancey and his brother in custody and that we had killed eight of the gang they were meeting. We were in pursuit of the rest and if possible, he might send a patrol in this direction and that you would find them."

Tye didn't say anything, just nodded his head and finished filling his canteen from the shallow pool formed by the spring. After they filled the canteens, water jug, and let the prisoners drink their fill, they let the horses in to drink. Yancey and Billy were quite except for Yancey's moaning from the injuries he received when 'he fell off his horse.' Tye, walking away said over his shoulder, "I'll be back in a few minutes, Lieutenant."

"Where are you going?"

"To do some thinking and try to figure out the best thing to do." Tye replied as he continued walking toward a cliff that overlooked the Rio Grande River. He walked to the edge of the cliff and sat down, looking down at the water which was forty feet below him. He looked across the river to the cliff on the other side which was Mexico. 'I really don't think they will head to Mexico,' he thought to himself. 'We hurt them pretty bad but they know we are way short on firepower.' Before, at times like this, he put himself in whoever's place he was chasing to see what he would do. Most of the time he had been right; with this bunch, if he guessed wrong...he didn't want to think about that. He stood up and walked back to an anxious Garrison.

"We have Yancey and Billy and they know we are short handed. I think they will come to get them."

"What do you suggest we do then?"

"Go back to the Freeman's homestead and fort up," Tye answered. "We can make a stand there and hope that we can hold out till help arrives."

"How long do you think that will be?" Christian asked.

"If Roberts makes it to the fort by in the morning and Thurston acts promptly to Lieutenant Garrisons request, I figure maybe noon or so the day after tomorrow."

"So how much time do we have before they come to get those two?" Garrison asked nodding toward the Cates brothers.

"Let's take things one at a time, Lieutenant. Let's get to the homestead and get our defense set up, and then I'll scout out things and see if I can find the answer to that question," Tye replied.

Traveling through the country with no trail to follow, Garrison was one lost puppy. They were traveling northwest, then east, back north, and who knows what other direction, following gulleys, crossing mesas, and then in mesquite so thick you couldn't see fifty feet. When they did arrive at the homestead, Garrison was once again amazed at how Tye and men like him, could find their way around the country. Arriving at the homestead, Tye again appreciated the location old man Freeman had selected. The cliff that overlooked the Pecos River was behind the house and the cliff overlooking the Rio Grande was on the left side of the house. Trouble could come from only two directions... unless the attackers were part mountain goat.

Tye and Christian found a large, heavy, three foot long log and carried it into the rear room of the homestead. They would use it to tie the horses' reins to, so they would not have to worry about them. They left the saddles on but loosened the girths. They may have to leave in a hurry and would only have to spend three or fours seconds tightening it back rather than have to re-saddle their mounts.

Tye and Christian then helped Garrison who was bringing rocks to block the front door. They would use the rear door which was close to the cliff overlooking the Pecos River to enter and leave the homestead. There were two windows in the front and one on each side of the building. Tye figured one man on each of the front windows and one on the window on the side away from the cliff would work. Tye had them pile a bunch of dry wood in two large stacks about thirty feet in front of the home. Tye soaked the wood with kerosene they found inside the home. Garrison and Christian wondered why but didn't ask.

A roof had not been added yet so Garrison lit a fire inside and boiled water to make some coffee. Christian took a bucket he found as well as the canteens and found a way down to the river to get water. He watered the horses, then made another trip to refill the bucket. They had forted up the homestead as well as they could. They had water and food available for at least two days even if they could not get back to the river. The prisoners were securely tied and a bandana stuffed in their mouths to keep them quiet. Tye felt they were ready so he tightened the girth on Sandy and led him out the back door to see if he could locate the men that he felt certain would be looking for them. He figured he had two hours left before it was full dark.

~~~

Curt, Joe, and Jake had been sent ahead by Lance to see if they could find any sign of the soldier boys. Curley and Dale had tried fixing up Vince's and Steve's shoulder wounds. Vince would be fine in a couple days as the bullet went through without hitting bone. Steve wasn't so lucky. The
~~~

bullet had shattered his collar bone and was still in the shoulder somewhere and needed to come out.

"You ever dig lead out of anyone Dale?" Lance, who had been watching them, asked.

"Once, got it out okay, but the man died anyway. We waited too long and infection got him."

"I watched plenty Yankee bullets removed after the fight at Vicksburg." Curley added.

"It's gonna be close now as to where the infection has set in or not. If'n we're gonna do anything we need to do it now." Dale said.

"You two get things ready and I'll start a fire." Lance ordered.

Dale and Curley got a couple shirts out of Steve's saddlebag and cut them into strips. Dale sharpened his knife on a rock and placed the blade in the fire that Lance had started. Once the blade was glowing red he told Curley to hold Steve as still as possible. Steve's eyes and facial features expressed his fear. Sweat was rolling off his forehead. His teeth ground against each other when the point of the blade entered the hole and started its probing. It hurt like hell but no sound came from Steve.

"FOUND IT!" Dale shouted excitedly. He stuck his finger in the hold and pulled the piece of lead out. Steve had passed out before Dale found the bullet. Dale placed the knife back in the fire.

"Pour some whiskey on the wound, Curley."

As soon as the knife was glowing red again, he took the flat side and scraped it across the hole. The blade melted the flesh, sealing up the wound.

"That's all we can do." Dale said. "We'll have to wait to find out about the infection."

"Good job, both of you," Lance said. "Now, fix up Vince's wound while we wait on the others to come back."

~~~
~~~

Tye was about two miles from the homestead when he topped a hill and pulled Sandy up sharply.

"Damn!" he exclaimed and turned Sandy around and left at a dead run as bullets whizzed all around him. When he had topped the hill he was face to face with the three men looking for him. They were less than fifty yards away when they seen each other. Sandy was putting some distance between them making Tye thankful for his speed.

Mesquites, cactus, and rocks were just a blur as Sandy sped toward the homestead. Tye gave him his head and Sandy knew where he was going. He topped a hill and was less than a hundred yards from the homestead when he slowed Sandy down and chanced a look over his shoulder. The riders were about a hundred fifty yards away and coming fast. 'Good,' Tye thought to himself. 'Keep coming. Just keep coming.' He passed the homestead and by the time he was dismounted and leading Sandy inside the riders were fifty to seventy five yards away. Rifle blast from the windows cart wheeled one of the riders off his horse and the others split off to the sides into the brush.

"Curt, can you see Joe?" Jake hollered.

"Yeah," Curt hollered. "He's deader than a damn hunk of old wood. What are we gonna do?"

"You stay here and make sure they don't leave. I'm gonna get Lance and the others. I should be back before midnight."

"Get your ass moving then."

~~~

"What the hell is going on, Tye?" Tye laughed, sat down and took his hat off and wiped the sweat off his forehead with his sleeve.

"Just thought I'd bring you boys a present."
~~~

"Well you could have given us a little warning." Christian said.

"Wouldn't have been a surprise then, would it?" Tye replied smiling. "I bumped into them a couple miles from here. Glad you boys were alert."

"Who wouldn't have been?" Garrison stated. "Sounded like a damn war was coming our way."

"What's the plan now, Sir?" Christian asked Garrison. There was a moment of silence as Garrison glanced at Tye, wanting help because he didn't have a damn clue except for the men to come in shooting.

"Let's get something to eat and some coffee," Tye said. "It will be awhile before they try anything. I'm sure one of them is out there waiting to pick one of us off if we show ourselves and the other is going to get the rest of them."

"Hell, there will be at least two or three of them to each of us." Christian said excitedly. Tye put his hand on Christian's shoulder.

"It ain't over yet, private. Maybe we can have a surprise for them when they come. Now let's get some grub and coffee." He turned and walked to the back room where the fire was, careful to stay out of sight of anyone looking thru the windows.

"What's he talking about, Lieutenant? How in the hell can three of us have a surprise for them?" Christian whispered.

"You know Tye as well as I do, private. He thinks like an Apache and very few times will you get an Apache in a trap. Just wait."

A few minutes later, eating a biscuit and drinking coffee, Tye eased back into the front room, making sure to duck under the windows so as not to give a target.

"As soon as full dark sets in, I'm going out the back door and over the cliff. I'll work my way around to where I can come up the cliff behind where they will be. When the shooting starts, we should have them in a crossfire."

"It's going to be dark as sin in awhile. How are we going to see them coming in?" Garrison asked. "There won't be a moon tonight you know."

"You will have these torches," Tye said showing the two sticks with rags wrapped around the end and soaked in kerosene. "When it's time, you can throw them into the stacks of wood. The yard should light up like its daylight."

Christian and Garrison looked at each other and smiled. "Sorta wondered about those stacks." Christian said.

"Now you know," Tye replied sipping on his coffee.

"When do we fire them?" Garrison asked.

"When the first shot is fired. It will probably be mine." Tye answered. "Let's get some rest. It's going to be a long night. I'll watch for awhile while you two get some sleep." Tye made his way to one of the front windows, making sure he stayed in the shadows. They were in a tight for sure. He wasn't so sure his plan would work but it was the only one he could come up with right now. These men were not pilgrims but were battle tested veterans. They were going to need all the luck they could get to escape this bunch of murdering bastards.

The only good thing that's happened lately is that the Cates boys have shut up. Since Tye threatened them awhile back, they haven't had much to say. Billy wasn't complaining about his wound anymore and Yancey didn't want to give Tye a reason to beat the hell out of him… again.

Chapter Eleven

Roberts had ridden hard to get back to the fort and had arrived much faster than expected. He knew the problem the men he had left were facing and had taken actions to speed things up. He had strapped the bodies more securely to their horses than they had at first. He and Arnold were riding double with a rope around both to keep Arnold, who was weak from loss of blood and only semi conscious at times, from falling off. They switched horses three times so they would have a fairly fresh mount under them all the time.

Arriving at the fort, he made his way directly to Thurston's office. It so happened that Thurston was on the porch of headquarters and saw him coming.

Running toward Roberts he grabbed the reins, stopping the horse. Roberts untied the rope and held the now unconscious Arnold till Thurston helped him off the horse. Roberts slid off the horse and staggered around to where Thurston was. Thurston had already ordered some men to help with Arnold and the dead men.

"You gotta send help, Sir!" Roberts said falling into the major's arms. Thurston gently laid him on the ground.

"Send help... where?"

"Toward where the Pecos and Rio Grande meet...only three men le...left, Sir. They are tr...trying to ca...catch up with tho...those murdering sonofa... Dispatch i...in m...my poc...pocket," he said, struggling to say conscious. Thurston pulled the dispatch from Roberts's pocket.

Thurston stood up and grabbed a nearby private by the shoulder, scaring the hell out the young soldier.

"YOU...PRIVATE... GO FIND CAPTAIN MCCLELLAN...NOW," Thurston shouted.

"Y...Yes, Sir," the startled private said. Thurston told others to help these troopers to the hospital. He headed to his office. He had barely gotten there when Captain McClellan came in.

"You send for me, Sir?" he asked while saluting. Thurston did not return the salute but turned toward the wall map. "Come over here, Captain." He pointed to an area on the map. "You are familiar with that area aren't you, Captain?"

"Yes Sir. Led three or four patrols around there."

"I need you to get a patrol together right now...in thirty minutes."

"Yes Sir. May I ask what is going on?"

"Get your patrol together and meet me outside in thirty minutes and I will explain everything. Right now I have to get the quartermaster to get some supplies for you in a hurry. Now get going. McClellan saluted and received a half salute from Thurston who was hurrying out of his office. McClellan headed toward O'Malley's to tell him to get a patrol ready. He wondered what in the hell was going on. He heard about the dead troopers and the injured Roberts and Arnold and knew something was wrong...big time wrong.

Thurston opened the dispatch from Garrison. It was a note written in a hurry, without the usual formalities.

Major Thurston:

As you probably know from Roberts, we have suffered severe losses but so have the men *we are after. They are down to about eight or nine from the twenty or so they had. I believe two of the eight are wounded. We are down to three, Tye, Private Christian, and myself. Please send a patrol due west from Fort Clark to the Rio Grande River and have them follow it toward the junction of the Pecos with all haste. Tell them to be alert as the men we are after are all ex-soldiers, probably confederate, and they hate the Union Army. They would not hesitate to ambush them if they have a chance. We have the Cates brothers in custody.*

Lieutenant Garrison.

Thurston hollered for his orderly and he came running. "Go to the quartermaster and give him this note from me."

"Yes sir," The orderly said saluting and left in a dead run with the note. He was with the quartermaster in three minutes. Sergeant Dante looked at the note and his butt was moving immediately, shouting orders for so and so to get this and so and so to get that. He looked at the note again.

Sergeant Dante—need supplies for a fifteen man patrol. Provisions for five days for men and horses; need thirty rounds of ammunition for each man. Please rush as they will be leaving immediately.

Major Thurston

'The old man could have given me a little more time,' he was thinking to himself. Dante ran an efficient warehouse and the supplies were ready when Captain McClellan came checking on them.

"Your food, cooking equipment, and even medical supplies I got from 'Old Sawbones' are on the packhorse. Full canteens and thirty rounds of ammunition in each belt are over here."

"Good job, Sergeant," McClellan said shaking the man's hand. "That has to be some kind of record."

"Is for me, Sir," Dante answered laughing. "Supplies for fifteen men and horses for five days in twenty minutes. Yes sir, got to be a record."

McClellan, with two troopers that were with him, brought the pack horse and ammo belts to the stables. Arriving there, he found O'Malley had the patrol ready. Five minutes later they were in front of headquarters, facing Thurston. Thurston and McClellan walked off to one side, away from the men.

"Lieutenant Garrison, Scout Watkins, and Private Christian have the two Cates boys, leaders of the gang that robbed the saloon in Brackett, in custody," Thurston said. "The problem is, the Cates were meeting a gang of about twenty or so hardcases. These men are probably ex-confederate soldiers that hate the Union. They, along with the Cates, have killed five soldiers in the last few hours and an unknown number of civilians. They have wounded two more soldiers, Corporal Arnold and private Roberts. In the skirmish, all but eight or nine of the gang were killed. You are to travel west to the Rio Grande and travel toward the junction of the Pecos. You should run into the gang or Lieutenant Garrison. Tell your scout that these men are ex-confederate soldiers and are ruthless. They know what they are doing, so be careful."

"Yes, Sir," McClellan said saluting. Thurston returned his salute; McClellan turned and walked to the men. "Get them mounted, Sergeant."

"Yes, Sir," Sergeant Norwood answered. He turned to the men who were standing by their mounts. "PREPARE TO MOUNT," he commanded and the men turned as one, placed their left foot in the stirup and their left hand on the pommel of the saddle. "MOUNT." Came the order and each man was in the saddle in a couple of seconds. "Ready Sir," Norwood said.

"By the two's then Sergeant," McClellan said taking his place in front.

"BY THE TWO'S...YO," Norwood said, and then pumping his arm up and down shouted, "DOUBLE TIME." The men formed two abreast and were at a fast trot when they crossed the bridge over Los Moras and hit the Old Mail Road turning left, toward the Rio Grande. The hollow sound the horses' hooves made striking the wooden planks of the bridge was loud and a few patrons of the saloon in Brackett came out to see what was going on and waving at the troopers.

'It feels good to be back in the saddle again,' McClellan was thinking to himself. He hadn't been on patrol in almost two weeks. He began to think the stupid stunt he had pulled a few weeks ago had made Thurston think twice about sending him back out. He thought back about a month or so when his whole outlook on things changed, especially about Tye. Untill that last patrol he could not stand Tye or the way the men looked up to him. He had to listen to the other officers' talk about him like he was some sort of Godsend to them. On the last patrol he stupidly led his men into an ambush and got several killed. They all would have been if it hadn't been for Tye saving their butts. He took a hard look at himself. He realized his feelings toward Tye were nothing but pure jealousy. The men loved him and respected him. Something they didn't for him. Before Tye arrived he had been seeing Rebecca and thought they had a future. Then, Tye stepped into the picture and he was out. He had never given any respect for Tye and who he was and what he did, that he deserved. When Tye pulled him and his men out of that deathtrap, he was a mental wreck. That was the first time he had been in a fight with the Apache. Tye took him aside and sat him down, away from the men. He told him the men had seen how he handled himself in the fight and they knew he had sand. He also told him a few things as to what it took to be respected by the troops. He was going to make mistakes, everyone does, but you go forward and never let the men see you out of control emotionly. He was a career man and the ambush he had led his men into would be on his record, not helping him in any way, but Tye didn't report it. He had told Thurston himself. Anyway, he had learned to respect Tye now for what he was and they had become friends.

~~~

It was almost full dark when Tye prepared to leave out the back of the homestead. There would be no moon tonight and he wanted to get down the cliff and find a way up the cliff behind where he figured the gang would be when they arrived before full dark.

"Remember to wait for my shot. Don't expose yourself if you can help it. They are loaded for bear and being ole boys from the South, are probably crack shots. As soon as I fire, light the torches and throw them into the wood pile. You should be able to see anyone approaching the house. Stuff something in those two mouths," pointing to the Cates. "Wouldn't want them to warn their friends. Good luck;" and he was gone.

"Think this is gonna work, Lieutenant?" Christian asked watching Tye disappear out the back door.

"If it don't, we won't have to worry about it…or anything else," Garrison answered. "Let's get to the windows and keep a watch. Have your torch and matches ready." They moved to the windows in front of the house.

Tye had managed to reach the floor of the canyon where the Pecos flowed and moved to his left along the base of the cliff. When he found where the cliff turned left again he was on the bank of the Rio Grande. It was now darker than sin and Tye wished he had left a few minutes earlier. He could only see a few feet right now but knew when his eyes grew a little more accustomed to the dark; he would see a little better. He stopped to rest and listen. He figured he had gone far enough to be behind them so he started looking for a way up the forty or so foot cliff.

The night was still and any sound he made would be magnified in this canyon. The only sound one could hear was the gurgling of the water over the rocks and the croaking of the frogs. He was climbing slow, careful of loose rocks that
~~~

would betray him. He was almost to the rim when he heard them. Several horses trotting on the rocky ground was pretty loud. He took advantage of the noise to scramble over the rim and find a hiding place. He heard the one who had stayed behind acknowledge the arrivals.

"Glad you boys decided to show up."

"Are they still in the house?" Lance asked.

"Unless they can fly," Curt said laughing. "Gonna be like shooting fish in a barrel."

"Ain't gonna be as easy as that. These fish can shoot back," Jake said. "Mabee so," Curly said, "but they killed Joe and I'm gonna take particular pleasure in killing them."

The men dismounted and walked over to where Jake was. Dale and Curt set up a picket line for the horses. Lance sat down on a large rock.

"We're gonna be here for awhile boys, so lets get comfortable," Lance stated as he laid back on the flat rock. "Jake, get a fire going and put us some coffee on."

"COFFEE!" Jake hollered. "This ain't no damn party, Lance. We're fixing to kill some fellers and probably some of us are gonna die," he bellowed.

"Pull your damn horns in, Jake," Dale hollered as Lance was getting up to settle things the only way he knew…with violence.

"Okay, Okay," Jake said looking at Lance. Lance sat back down on the rock, glad he didn't have to kill Jake. He would probably need him before this was over.

Tye was watching and listening to everything that was said. What he heard only convinced him that this was the worst bunch he had ever encountered. Listening to the argument, he was hoping they would get into a fight and one, or maybe both, would die lowering the odds a little. His heart stopped as one of the men was walking directly toward him telling the others he needed to take a leak... There was nowhere for Tye to go. If he moved he would probably be seen… and then, he would surely die.

Chapter Twelve

Tye held his breath, not even blinking as the man looked around as he relieved himself. Tye finally breathed again when the man finished and returned to the others. Tye cursed his bad luck when the men suddenly spread out and started toward him. Evidently, the man had saw Tye and did a good job of pretending not to have.

"WHOEVER YOU ARE...STAND UP WITH YOUR HANDS EMPTY!" Lance shouted. Tye lay still for a couple seconds then slowly stood up.

"WALK TO US...SLOWLY," Lance ordered. Tye started toward them, his mind working furiously, trying to figure a way out of this mess. He knew he was in for some pain and probably facing the fact these murdering bastards would kill him. He walked slowly.

"What happened?" Christian whispered.

"I think they discovered Tye."

"Damn," Christian mumbled. "What the hell are we going to do now?" He said, his trembling voice betraying his fear...

"Settle down first. Let me think." Garrison replied. They could now see the men walking around the campfire. Suddenly, they saw Tye thrown rougly to the ground, his hands tied behind his back. One of the men stood him up and another buried his fist in Tye's stomach and then caught Tye in the face with his knee when Tye doubled over. Tye was stood up again, and again a fist in the belly left him lying in the dirt. The men were taunting Tye and laughing.

"Sonofabitches!" Christian hollered

"ALL OF YOU SHUT UP!" Lance hollered. The men were immediately quiet.

"Any of you know who the hell this man is?"

Looking around, Dale answered. "Nope; but from his clothes, he's either military or a scout."

"Big sonofabitch ain't he?" Curly commented.

"Could be that scout everyone talks about," Curt said.

"Who's that?" Lance questioned.

"Tye Watkins." Curt answered.

"Heard about him," Dale said. "Supposed to be the best there is."

"Well, he don't look none to tough now," Dale said laughing.

"Check the rope on his hands." Lance said looking at Dale. "We'll find out who he is when he comes around." He picked up a cup of coffee and sat down. "We still have at least two men in that homestead. That's our immediate problem."

"It's dark, let's just rush 'em and get it over with and then come back and kill this one," Jake said.

"You go ahead, Jake. Try your luck. They already killed mor'n half of us. They ain't gonna fold up their tent and surrender. They are soldiers and one of them is probably an officer." Looking at Jake, who hadn't moved, Lance asked, "Whatcha waiting for Jake? Go ahead and rush 'em."

Jake looked around and saw he would be alone. "I'll wait," he muttered quietly.

"Good idea, Jake. Now all of you get some coffee while I sort things out."

Garrison and Christian could not hear every word but enough to know they had to do something quick. They could see Tye lying on his stomach, not moving, just to the left of where the men were sitting, drinking their coffee.

"Sitting there like a damn bunch of vultures...just waiting," Christian mumbled to himself but loud enough for Garrison to hear.

"Got an idea," Garrison said.

"If'n you do, I'm all ears cause I sure as hell don't." Christian whispered.

"Let's take the fight to them."

"You crazy, Lieutenant?"

"Listen. We're dead if we stay here. They can wait till daylight and come from two directions. Remember, they have repeaters and we have these single shot Spencers. They have enough fire power to keep our heads down while they over run us. Who knows if Roberts got to the fort and even if he did, it would probably be late tomorrow before any help arrives."

"What about Tye? He's dead meat if we start shooting."

"We are going to sneak up close, from two sides and open up with our rifles and then our pistols. Maybe in the confusion, Tye can get away."

"Sounds like a long shot to me."

"You got a better idea?"

"No, Sir."

"Then get ready."

Tye had regained his senses and lay still, listening, pretending to still be out. What he heard sent chills up his spine. These men talked about killing and raping as easy as talking about the weather. They talked freely, laughing about the people at the homestead they had killed; about the rapes of the women and young girls. The cold, un-feeling way they talked made Tye sick. How in hell could anyone be that calloused was beyond him. He was worried about Garrison and Christian. They were in a pickle and he was of no use. He hoped his thought about Garrison having a good head on his shoulders panned out and Garrison did something to get himself and Christian out. He then thought of Rebecca. The thought of him never seeing her again, of never holding her again overwhelmed him and he got a lump in his throat. What would she do? He remembered Buff, thankful he was there to take care of her. He lay there thinking of all these things and all the hate he had for these men and men like them gave him new strength. He wasn't going to die without a fight. He begain to fight the ropes binding his hands, hurting like hell; he could feel the wetness of the blood that was beginning to come from the ropes sawing into his wrists.

His eyes went beyond the light of the fire toward the homestead. He was shocked to see Garrison behind a small sage, looking directly at him. Looking quickly at the men, he was relieved that none of them was paying attention to the homestead. Tye nodded at Garrison, acknowledging that he was ready for whatever the Lieutenant had in mind. Tye waited...watching. He then saw Christian, about thirty yards to the left.

At that time, Lance stood up. "This is what we are gonna do. At first light, the sun will be behind our backs. All of you know a man can't shoot straight looking into the sun. It will be..."he didn't finish as Garrison shot him square in the chest, knocking him backwards into the fire. He screamed, tried to get up but fell flat on his face, dead. All the men jumped up, pulling their guns. Christian shot the one who had done most of the bragging right between the eyes. Then all hell broke loose. Tye was rolling into the brush with the first shot, gained his feet, and was running, circling to where he last saw Garrison.

Garrison and Christian were firing their pistols as fast as they could. Two more men were down and the others firing the repeating rifles as fast as they could lever in shells. Garrison and Christian hugged the ground as the bullets were thick above them covering them with mesquite branches that were being splintered by the bullets. The men, when their rifles were empty, found their horses and skedadling away as fast as they could, firing blindly behind them with their pistols.

"LIEUTENANT!" Tye called when he saw Garrison. "IT'S ME, TYE."

"TYE," Garrison said excitedly. "Boy, I'm thankful you are okay."

"Only half as much as I am," Tye said smiling. "Is Christian okay?"

"I'm fine," Christian said coming from behind a mesquite.

"Check the men in the camp, Christian. Make sure they are dead," Garrison ordered.

"Yes, Sir, Lieutenant."

"Let's get those ropes off your hands, Tye." A shot startled both of them. "Christian, you okay?" Tye asked.

"Yes, Sir. One was still alive...he's dead now." Garrison looked at Tye. Tye shrugged. "If you knew those men like I know them you would not even think twice about him killing one of them. I listened to them talking about killing the Freemans and raping the women and girls and was laughing about it. They are mean, Lieutenant. As mean as I have ever seen," Tye said as they walked to the fire and Christian. "Get out of the light from the fire, Christian," Tye said. "You make a tempting target standing there." Christian realizing what Tye was saying was true, moved quickly to the outside of the firelight.

"You two saved my hide tonight, Lieutenant," Tye said shaking each man's hand.

"That's a first," Christian said laughing. "Wait till the boys back at Clark hears someone saved your butt for a change." They all laughed and Tye grabbed his side.

"Musta bruised a rib," he said grimacing.

"Your nose looks busted too," Garrison added.

"Ain't nothing compared to what they was fixing to do to me. Thanks again."

"DAMN!" Garrison exclaimed. "I plumb forgot about the Cates. Christian, go bring them here."

"Yes, Sir. Be right back."

"Got some bandages in my saddle bag, Tye. When Christian gets back, I'll see what I can do for you."

A shout from Christian startled them both. "THE SUMBITCHES ARE GONE." Tye and Garrison looked at each other and began running to the homestead. They found Christian holding the ropes they had been bound with covered with blood.

"Dammit, Christian. I told you…" Tye cut Garrison off.

"What's done is done. No use crying over it. We'll get 'em."

"Yeah, I know. But how many more innocent homesteaders will die till then?"

Tye just shook his head. "We'll get 'em. It's too dark to track anyone now. I think we ought to head back and see if we can find the patrol."

"If Roberts got to the Fort." Christian commented.

"He got there. I know Roberts well," Garrison said.

"Let's get mounted and get out of here." Tye said.

"What about the bodies?" Garrison said.

"Would they have buried us? Let the coyotes and the buzzards have them." Tye said, thinking of what these men had done to the Freemans. "Let's find a place to camp and then find the patrol in the morning."

~~~

"Come on Billy," Yancey hollered. Billy was lagging behind as Yancy and he were scrambling through the sage, rocks, and mesquites in a effort to put distance between themselves and the soldiers.

"Dammit, I'm doing the best I can." Billy screamed back at Yancey. "My damn shoulder is killing me."

"If we can't get away from that stinking Watkins, you won't have to worry none about your shoulder 'cause your neck is gonna be stretched some." Billy didn't answer but did pick up the pace some. When they were back at the homestead, Yancey had been struggling with the ropes binding his hands resulting in them bleeding. The blood,
~~~

mixed with the sweat on his arms, had allowed him to finally slip them. Untying Billy, they slipped out the back of the homestead while the fight was going on. They were now about a mile from the homestead moving along the banks of the Rio Grande.

"There was a lot of shots fired," Billy commented as they took a short breather. "Who do you think survived, the boys are the soldiers?"

Yancey thought for a couple seconds before answering. "I figure Lance and the others took some losses. Those blue coates know their business and you add that damn Watkins and you have problems." He thought about the scout and the beating he had received from him and his blood boiled. "I'm gonna kill that bastard and I'm gonna take some enjoyment from it."

Their eyes had adjusted some what to the darkness but seeing more than a few feet was impossible. The river here was slow moving with no sound except the gurgling noise where a big boulder split the current. A splash every once in a while was heard as a fish took a meal on the surface and the mournful howl of a lonely coyote could be heard. The only other sound was the buzzing of the ever present insects including the pesky mosquitos.

"Put some of this on your face, neck, and hands," Yancey said, handing Billy some mud from the bank. "It will keep the insects off." Billy took the mud and applied it thick on his exposed skin.

"Are we gonna be able to meet up with the boys?" Billy asked.

"Mabee. Don't really care if we do or not."

"Why do you say that?"

"I got one goal right now and that's to get Watkins for what he did to me. First though, we need to find us a homestead so we can get some weapons and horses."

~~~
~~~

"What are we gonna do?" Jake asked while giving his horse a drink from his hat.

Dale, standing by his mount, looked at Jake. "We'll do what we were gonna do before. We'll find us some homesteaders and kill'um. Maybe even find us some women. Besides, if there's any loot, there ain't so many of us to share it now."

"Who made you the damn boss?" Curt asked. "Far as I'm concerned this idea that Lance and Yancey had of getting rich by killing and robbing these homesteaders is over. From what I've seen so far, the reward ain't worth the risk. Damn people out here ain't got any more than us...which if you ain't checked lately, is nothing except what's on our backs."

"Ain't ever had nothing my whole life any way," Dale replied. "As far as my running things, never intended to. Jake just asked a question and I answered it. You can stay with us or leave, makes no matter to me either way."

"Things ain't the way they were," Jake chimed in. "Most our friends are dead or headed for a hanging. I just want to get some sleep and forget these damn homesteaders out here and head back to Georgia in the morning."

"Same here," Curt said.

"If that's the way ya'll feel, then let's get a fire started, make a little coffee, get some rest, then start back early," Dale suggested.

"What about the soldiers and Watkins?" Jake asked.

"Damn, Jake," Curt said. "Look around. A damn Apache couldn't track anything tonight it's so dark." They were probably three miles from the homestead; just a short ways from a low cliff that over looked the Rio Grande. In a few minutes they were drinking coffee. There was no talk as each was thinking the same thing; events of today that killed most of their friends and of getting out of this country and heading home. A few minutes later, with the fire burning down, they turned in, depending on their horses to alert them to anyone or anything coming close to the camp.

~~~

Tye, Garrison, and Christian only went far enough away from the homestead to where Tye felt comfortable there would be no surprises from the men who had escaped the fight and from the Cates. Tye looked at the position of the stars and figured it was almost midnight as they shook out their bedrolls and prepared to get some sleep.

"You could have picked a place that wasn't so damn rocky," Christian said as he sat back up removed a rock that had been sticking him in the back.

"Hard to find a place that's perfect. Everything in this land can scratch, sting, or stick you," Tye answered laughing.

"You two shut up and get some sleep," Garrison ordered. When lying in his bedroll, Tye's thoughts always went toward Rebecca, wondering what she was doing. He lay back and looked at the stars remembering her warm embrace, her tender kisses. He was thankful that Buff was with her, especially now that these white marauders were on the loose. They could enter the fort fairly easily and take her. God, he missed her.

~~~

"Up sorta late ain't ya, Rebecca?" Buff asked as Rebecca came out on the porch where he was sitting. She had a shawl across her shoulders to keep away the chill of the night air. The air was crisp and had the smell of rain even though there were no clouds.

"I couldn't sleep, Buff. I was wondering what Tye was doing right now and where he was…and if he's okay."

"Snug in his bedroll and thinking uf yu, if I wus gessing." Rebecca laughed. "You always say the right things to make me feel better. I just had this feeling that he was hurt and needed me."

"Rebecca, tha thar man of yurs luves ya mor'n life it's self. Thar's nuthin in this heer ole world tha wud keep him frum cumin bac ta yu. I'm shor Ben wus tha way with his wife Lori."

"He got himself killed."

"Shor he did but not fur years uf cumin bac to her afta meeny fites with tha 'patches and tha bandits. Lori an Ben had manee a gud years together afore he got himself kilt. Yu and tha thar man uf yurs are gonna have manee uf them also."

She sat down on the porch beside Buff and put her head on his shoulder. "I know he can take care of himself but like Ben, he will endanger himself trying to help others. That's what got Ben killed."

"So I hurd. His job is ta make this heer land a safe plac fur uthers ta live. That wus whut Ben wus doing when he got himself kilt. If'n sumda it happn's ta Tye, yu can live with tha fact tha he died duing whut he luved, what he tho't wus tha rite thang tu do ta make this heer land a safur plac fur yu and me. Frum whut I've hurd abut him, thar's nuthin fur yu ta wurry yur purty hed abut. He kan mor'n take care of his own self."

"I know you said you never went to school, never learned to read or write, but you have the ability to always know just what to say to a person to make them feel better when they are feeling low. That makes you a very smart, special man in my eyes. Thank you." She put her head back on his shoulder and shivered slightly from the cool night air.

"Rebecca."

"What is it, Buff?"

"Are we gonna keep havin these heer konvusation abut Tye ever nite?"

Rebecca laughed. "Now that you mention it, I think we are. You just do a good job of making a lonesome girl feel better."

"Yu bett'r git yourself bac in tha house afor' yu git yurslf sick." He stood up and helped her get up. He held the door open for her when she went it.

"A gentlemen too," she said smiling. "Goodnight, Buff."

"Gudnite Rebecca." He sat back down on the porch and looked up at the night sky. "Heer tha Ben. Furst time I ev'r been kalled smart an a gentamen. Bet ya wud nev'r gast tha wud have been sade abut me." He laughed, sat for a few minutes then stood up and went inside to go to bed.

Chapter Thirteen

Long before the sun made its appearance, Tye and the others were saddled and moving out, hoping to find the patrol. Tye was concerned that there were three groups of men besides themselves somewhere in the area and two of them were not who he wanted to find... just yet. He was concerned that the Cates might have found a homestead and now have some firepower. They were the most dangerous of the two groups. Yancey was smart and had no qualms about killing anyone. The other group he figured was in disarray since the big man that was doing all the talking before the fight was dead. He figured he had been the leader of this bunch of .... He paused trying to think of what to call them because they were certaintly not men...animals' maybe, but not men.

The only sound breaking the early morning silence was the horse's hooves striking the rocks as the three men rode south. The river was on their right, about a quarter of a mile away. A deep canyon ran parallel to them less than a half mile to their left. That didn't leave a lot of room for the groups of men to maneuver without running into each other. Tye pulled up Sandy suddenly and Garrison's horse almost bumped into him.

"What is it, Tye?"

"Fresh tracks," Tye answered. "Keep your mounts back for a minute." He dismounted to study the tracks closer; running his finger over the tracks and then standing up, looked south, where they were handing.

"Not more than an hour old, Lieutenant. They are headed the same direction we are and are not in a hurry." Tye mounted Sandy. "I think I should take a look ahead of us. You two come too but stay a hundred or so yards behind me. You damn cavalry men can't travel very quite with your spurs jingling and sabers rattling," he said smiling.

"We'll stay back," Garrison replied.

"Be ready for trouble. It could come in a hurry." Tye said as he rode off.

Garrison turned to Christian. "Take your rifle out of its scabbard and be ready."

"Yes Sir." Christian said taking the Sharps out, pointed the barrel toward the sky, the butt resting on his thigh and cocked.

~~~

Back at Fort Clark, Shakespeare and Rebecca was eating a hearty breakfast of eggs, bacon, and bisquits at the O'Malley's. Mrs. O'Malley had invited them to breakfast last night. Sergant O'Malley had just arrived after having to attend to early morning duties first.

"Anee wurd last night on Tye an tha patrol?" Shakespeare asked.

"Not a word, Buff." O'Malley said, concern showing in his voice. "Not a damn word." Buff looked at Rebecca and saw the fear of the unkown in her face and she was just picking at her food.

"I'm shor tha don't meen nuthing does it, Sergant?" Buff asked, winking at O'Malley and nodding toward Rebecca. O'Malley realized what Shakespeare mean't by the remark.

"No sir. Not hearing from a patrol every day is nothing unusual. Sometimes it can be days and days," he said looking at Rebecca.

"I'm okay you two. I just don't have much of an appetite," Rebecca said.
~~~

O'Malley decided to change the subject. "Who was the best of all the mountain men excluding yourself of course?" he asked.

Buff pushed his plate away and took a sip of coffee. "Jus depens on whu yu ask I guess. I seen them all, Bridger, Jim Baker, Joe Meek, Jedediah Smith, Joseph Walker, and even met Kit Carson once. Thar wure a hole lot more uf men whu were damn gud but nev'r noticed fur wun reeson or anuther. Tha smartest wus problee Smith. He wus educated an he wus mountain smart. Tha best fiter wus probably Tye's pa, Ben. Tha best trapp'ar wus Bridger. The best trailblazer was Walker and tha best injun fiter wus Baker or Carson. If'n yu take all tha thangs tha make up whut it tuk to be a monton man, trappin, fiting, traking, gud sense, and put them in to wun man, yu wuld have ta pick Ben Watkins. Nev'r seed him luse a standup-knockum down fest fite. He wus a ferst class trapp'r and mor'n held his own again' the Blackfut. He kud also reed and rite which wus mor'n most uf us kud do. My fren Bridger is tha best known and he wus gud...but he kud also tale storees bett'rn aneewun else. Ben wusn't much uf a talker. I got me a whole passel uf storees ta tale Tye abut his pa cause I kno Ben nev'r bragged on his own self.

"Always wondered about Carson?" O'Malley said questionally.

"He wus a prettie fare monton man but he kame in tha thirtees, just abut tha time tha beever craze wus slowing down. He made his mark as a injun fighter and skout fur Freemont. Havt'a say he wuz gud at both. I thank he wus like most famus men, storees wure based on fact but stretched sum by them eastern writers. Ain't takin nuthin away frum him though."

"What about you Buff? I heard stories about you too."

"Kinda like Ben when it cumes ta tootin' my own horn. I fell a little short uf sum but I wus better'n most I guess. I wuz in them montons far a lotta years and still have all my hare." He stood up and run his fingers through his silver hair. "All thar," he said. O'Malley reached over and patted the small man on the shoulders.

"Never liked anyone who tooted his own horn; I know that you were a much better mountain man than you say. Tye's told me stories about you that Ben told him. You were something else, Buff and I'm right proud to know you. I also know Tye is glad you are here to take care of Rebecca."

"As long as I'm breathing, I'll do that."

~~~

There was just enough breeze this morning to rustle the long thin leaves on the mesquite. The only other sound was Sandy's hooves when they struck a rock. Tye was alert, his eyes searching everywhere, looking for anything out of place, anything moving. He now knew how the fox felt entering the panthers den. The hairs on his neck were standing up and he could feel his heart pounding, like it was fixing to explode out of his chest. He was close to the bastards, he could feel it.

Glancing over his shoulder, he could see Garrison and Christian about two hundred yards back. Looking back in front he caught a glimpse of something flash from the sun. It was quick and only flashed once, he just happened to be looking or he would not have seen it. Standing in his stirrups, he surveyed the place where the flash came from. He wasn't concerned that the flash was from a rifle barrel or he might be in someone's sights. The flash was a quarter of mile away at least. He turned around in the saddle and motioned for the others to come on. He took the makings out and finished rolling a smoke just as they rode up.

"What is it, Tye?" Garrison asked excitedly.

"Dunno for sure. Got a glimpse of something reflecting the sun over younder about where that large rock is on the hill." Garrison stared at the rock for a full minute before saying anything.
~~~

"Nothing there now that I can see."

"May be nothing. Learned a long time ago though, there ain't too many things out here that reflects sunlight except man made things like rifles or silver buckles and stuff."

"What's the plan?"

Tye studied the terrain for a few seconds. The flash came from the top of a hill and where they were now, he could see no way to get there that offered any cover. "Spread out and let's go to the top of that hill. Be ready for anything and don't top the hill. I want to get a look on the other side before we get skylined." The three men, with Tye slightly in front, spread out and moved up the hill. The mesquite, sage, and large cactus were missing in this particular area which would have offered some protection. As it was, Tye knew they were in trouble if the men were there. With repeating rifles, they could lay down a murderous fire from the high ground.

All three men knew the situation was dangerous and each was sweating profusely even though the early morning was still fairly cool. Fifty yards from the top, Tye signaled the men to stop and motioned them to come to him. Looking around, he found what he was looking for.

"Lieutenant, why don't you and Christian dismount and get behind that boulder." He nodded toward a boulder that was probably three or four foot across and almost three foot high. "If you use that rock to steady your aim you can hit anyone that sticks his head up over that ridge."

"What are you going to do?" Lieutenant Garrison queried.

"See what I can find up there," Tye said as he dismounted and tied Sandy to a small sage brush. "Just fire at anything you see move ahead of me."

He moved off at a trot, changing direction every three or four steps. 'No use making it easy for anyone up there,' he thought to himself. His moccasin's barely made a sound on the rocky ground as he zig-zagged his way up the hill. Ten yards from the top, he stopped, dropped to the ground and listened. He thought he had heard a horse whinny but could not be sure. He lay there for a full minute, listening for any sound that wasn't normal.

Hearing nothing after a minute, he stood up slowly and then, in a crouch, made his way to the top. Reaching it, he dropped on the ground, took off his hat, and peered over. He had heard a horse. About two hundred yards down the opposite side of the ridge; he was looking at the backs of three men. He knew it was them because of the bright red jacket one man wore. He had thought last night when he was a prisoner and saw the man wearing it how stupid for a man to wear something like that out here. He could be seen from a mile away. He looked back at his friends and motioned for them to come on up.

"That's them alright," Christian said as he slid in beside Tye. He saw the man with the red jacket. "Not another man would wear something that stupid out here."

"What do you think we should do," Garrison asked.

"Nothing," Tye answered.

"Nothing! Why do you say that?" an astonished Garrison asked.

"For one thing there is no cover and we would be spotted immediately and be in for a long chase that could result in some bad things happening," Tye answered sharpley.

"Such as?"

"Lieutenant, have you ever been on a horse running full speed out here in this terrain?"

"Only at a gallop."

"I aint talking at a gallop, I'm talking all out, as fast as your horse can run."

"No, can't say I have other than by the fort."

"Four things can happen in a fire fight from a running horse and three of them are bad. First, the men you are chasing might get a lucky shot in and hit you or your horse. Second, your horse steps in a hole, goes down; his leg will probably be broken. Thirdly, if your horse goes down there's a hell of a good chance you will be hurt too, maybe killed. Look at the ground. Their tracks will be as plain as day. Even you could probably track them," Tye said smiling. A snicker came from Christian but he quickly got quite after the Lieutenant gave him a go to hell look.

"Let's play it safe and hang back a ways and wait for the right opportunity." They made their way back down to their horses, mounted and slowly made their way back up and over the ridge. The three men were out of sight and as Tye said, Garrison could see their tracks plain. They followed at a leisurely pace.

~~~

"Do we know where we are headed?" Curt asked.

"I don't have any damn idea," Jake answered, "But we don't have much of a choice do we. The damn canyon over there to our left has twenty to forty foot walls and on our right is the river and Mexico."

"And that stinking scout and the others are somewhere behind us," Dale added.

Curt turned in the saddle and looked behind them. Seeing nothing, he turned back in the saddle and stared straight ahead, seeing nothing as his brain was working, trying to figure out why in the hell he was in this mess. After the War, he had headed back home in Georgia to help his parents out. Everything was good until one day when his old friend he had soldiered with, Lance, had showed up. Lance was a talker and convinced him that farming wasn't for him, that there was land and money for the taking in Texas. Lance had some 'friends' that was going with him and sure wanted him to join them. Curt looked at his mother and father and saw how this life had aged them. The hard work and the elements had taken their toll. His pa was forty-one but looked way over fifty. He had said good-bye to his parents and remembering his mothers' tears as he rode away, put a lump in his throat. He
~~~

didn't realize just what kind of 'friends' Lance had gathered until it was too late and they had already killed and robbed several people. He had watched, but not participated in the rape of the young girls and women. He had taken a little 'hoo-rawing' from the men about that. All he wanted to do now was to get back home. His twentieth birthday would be in a month and a half and he sure would like to spend it back home.

"Don't know about you two but I'm hungrier than a bear coming out of hibernation," Dale muttered.

"Me too," Jake said. "Let's take a rest and chew some jerky."

'Jerky hell', Curt thought to himself. 'Ever since he had left home it seemed he had eaten nothing but jerky.' Dale was right though, it had been awhile since they had eaten and he was hungry enough that even the almost tasteless jerky sounded good. They dismounted and gave their mounts a drink before they sat down to chew some.

~~~

"We have to find something to eat, Yancy," an obviously exhausted Billy said as he collapsed to the ground. He was weak from hunger and loss of blood from his wound. "I can't go any farther."

Yancy sat down beside his brother and looked around for someplace Billy could rest out of the sun. "Stay here for a few minutes Billy, while I look around." He knew his brother had reached his limit. The only thing that surprised him was that Billy had come this far. He figured they had come five or six miles since they escaped last night. He climbed out of the river bank and looked around; looking for anyplace Billy could hide while he found something for them to eat. It didn't take him long to find what he was looking for. A thick stand of mesquite offered plenty of shade and protection from anyone seeing him.
~~~

He climbed back down the bank and helped Billy up. "I found a place for you to rest while I find us something to eat. Let's wash all this mud off and get a good drink before we start up the bank." A few minutes later, Billy was lying in the shade of a huge mesquite. "I'll be back as soon as I can," Yancy said. He smiled when he saw he was wasting his breath as Billy was sleeping soundly.

Yancy climbed a small hill to look around the area for any sign of life. He was elated to see a small herd of goats. He knew there would be a homestead close by. He sat down to watch and hadn't been there five minutes when a man appeared, walking toward the goats. The goats saw him and headed his way. As the man and the goats moved away from where Yancy was, Yancey stood up and begain following them. He walked less than a quarter mile when he saw the home...or what was supposed to be a home. He could tell by looking that these people didn't have anything. The house was a shanty and in need of a hell of lot of repair. He figured the only thing he was going to get here would be a small amount of food and that was a maybe.

Walking into the open he hollered at the man. "HELLO". The man, startled at the sound of a voice spun around and to Yancy's surprise, held a pistol in his hand. Yancy threw up his hands and with a big smile, started talking. "Don't want no trouble mister. Got myself throwed yesterday and lost my horse. Ain't had a thing to eat since yesterday...just looking for some food." The man saw Yancy had no weapon and reholstered his pistol.

"Don't have much but your welcome to what I have." The man turned to open the door and Yancy quickly closed the gap between them. By the time the man saw Yancy, it was too late. Yancy knocked him cold with a right that caught the man flush on the chin. Yancy picked up the pistol the man had attempted to draw. He stripped the belt and holster from him and walked into the house. The man had to live alone as no woman would keep a house this filthy. He found a knife, two cans of beans, and some coffee...and a sharps rifle. Digging around the filth he found a handful of cartridges for the rifle. Going outside he smelled a fire. Following his nose to the side of the house, he was estatic. Above a small fire, hung a hunk of meat on a spit that he figured was goat. It smelled as good as anything he had smelled before and he immediately cut off a slice with the knife. It was good and almost melted in his mouth. He took it off the fire but left it on the stick. He found a sack and put the coffee and beans it it. He strapped on the gunbelt, picked up the rifle, and walked out of the yard, anxious to get back to Billy. He glanced back at the man and saw he had not moved. If he had, he would have killed him. "Probably should anyway," he said outloud and stopped, started to turn around but thought about it for a second and decided to leave him be.

He found where he left Billy. His brother was still stretched out on the ground, sound asleep. He woke him up by holding a piece of the meat under his nose. Billy sat up quickly and grabbed a piece and wolfed it down. Yancey opened a can of beans with the knife and handed the can to Billy. Billy turned the can up and filled his mouth with the contents, bean juice running down his chin.

"Slow down, Billy. It ain't going nowhere so take your time."

"Where did you get this?"

"Homesteader about a half mile from here."

"Dead?"

"Nope. Must be getting soft in my old age," Yancy said laughing. It was good to laugh and see his brother laugh again. A couple days ago, it looked liked the laughing would never come around again. Thinking about a rope stretching your neck has that affect on a man. He laid down and fell asleep immediately.

Chapter Fourteen

For the last few hours, Tye had dogged the tracks of the three men. Like an Apache, he had managed to do this without being seen by them. As the sun was setting, it was getting time to do something. Spotting a large group of tracks coming from the southwest from the river, he dismounted to take a closer look in the fading light.

"DAMN," he cursed loudly, startling Garrison.

"What is it?"

"Apaches, and from the looks of these tracks, I would say about twenty-five or thirty."

"Apache. Where in hell did they come from?" Garrison queried.

"Not sure, Lieutenant. A few days ago, Dan and me were sent to a place on the Rio Grande where there had been a report of constant drums beating. We saw the largest group of Apache warriors I have ever hoped to never see. Musta been about two hundred-fifty warriors."

"TWO HUNDRED-FIFTY," Garrison said. "Are you sure?" he questioned.

"Dammit," Tye said disgustingly. "That's the same damn thing Thurston asked me. Do you think I would make something like that up?"

"Calm down, Tye. I didn't mean it that way but, that many warriors in one place is hard to believe. Lipan?"

"Yes, there were Lipan, Mescalero, Tonto, White Mountain, Jicarillo, and Chiricahua at the camp; maybe others too."

"I didn't know the different bands ever came together."

"Never have before," Tye replied.

"What are they doing here?" a nervous Christian said thinking of the twenty-five Apaches to three of them.

"I don't know why they are here but I know what they are now doing."

"Fill us in." Garrison said.

"Like I said a minute ago, I don't know where they come from or had in mind doing. Now, I know exactly what they are doing," Tye said mounting Sandy. "They crossed the tracks we were following and now they are following them too figuring on killing them and getting some weapons."

"That's great!" Christian said. "That's all we need to make this patrol compete…damn Apaches with repeating rifles."

Tye smiled. "They don't have them yet."

"I know that but if they do…"he paused for a second, "hell, I don't want to even think about it. Gives me the shivers."

"We were lucky that we were staying far enough behind them for the Apaches not to see us," Tye said.

"Amen to that," Garrison said.

"It's gonna be dark in thirty minutes, Lieutenant, I think we need to call it a day, make camp so we won't stumble onto them in the dark or accidently get close enough they hear the horses. Sound will carry a long ways out here and we ain't that far behind them to take a chance."

"What about the three men?" Garrison asked.

"Unless the Apaches catch them in the next few minutes they will wait until the morning. Apaches don't fight at night unless there's no other choice."

They turned to the right, toward the river to find a camp. "We can get some water and if they do stumble onto us, we'll have the steep bank to our rear and will only have to worry about them coming in from the front." They found a place just as it was starting to get dark when they reached the bank. Christian found a way down the bank and filled the water bag for the horses and each of their canteens.

"Cold camp tonight boys; no fire if you want to see another sunup." Tye said.

"Cold bisquits and water sounds good compared to the alternative," Christian said. After eating their 'meal' it was time to turn in with each man taking turns standing watch in two hour shifts. Christian took the first,

Lying on their bedrolls Tye and Garrison found sleep hard to come by even as tired as they were.

"Guess you're glad that Buff showed up after all these years?"

"More than anyone could ever know." Tye answered. "My pa was a man that never spoke much of his past. I knew what he had been because of my mom and the few stories I could get out of him. We spent more nights under the stars than in our homestead. That's where I got most of the stories from him. Most of them though were stories that had a meaning to them...you know like how to handle a similar situation if I got into one. Been a few of them that's come to past and I remembered his advice; saved my sorry hide more than once. Now Buff is here, and he can fill in all the blanks, answer all the questions that have haunted me for years about the truth and the stories about pa. Yeah, I'm more than happy he is here."

"He's a character, I'll say that."

"He's a part of the past, Lieutenant. He lived a life that no one will ever live again." Tye paused for a few seconds. "I'm very envious of him."

"Just watching him get around I'd never guess in a thousand years that he was seventy-one years old."

"He can still take care of himself, I'll guarantee you that." Tye rolled over on his side. "Let's get some sleep, Lieutenant."

Garrison lay there thinking of Ben and Buff and the time of the mountain men. He had read those stories about them but never figured he would ever meet one, neverless one that he had read about. 'I'm as anxious as Tye to hear those stories,' he thought. With that thought, he drifted off to sleep.

~~~

Curt, Dale, and Jake were lying in their bedrolls, talking about the last two days events. The chill of the night was taken away by a fire, a fire way to big not to be noticed. Most men out here knew better that to build a fire in the open and if they had to build one, it was small and in a hole with rocks around it to help keep it from prying eyes. The three men here ex-soldiers and were fighters but they were pilgrims when it came to understanding the way things were out here in this country. Men wore clothes and rode horses that did not stand out. There were very few white or black horses around. The only thing they did right was decide to alternate standing guard.

~~~

Nasay smiled when he saw the fire. He knew these men knew nothing of the Apache. He would kill them at first light tomorrow. He had twenty-five warriors with him. They were not young but were veteran warriors; warriors that knew the ways of the soldiers and warriors that had fought the Commache and the Kiowa. He led a dangerous group, not only to the three men in the camp Nasay was watching, but to the settlers and soldiers as well.

Twenty-six veteran Apache warriors was a formidable force to deal with. Nasay was a Mescalero Apache, one of the most vicious fighting bands of the Apache Nation. He was a long ways from his homeland. He and his men had attended the meeting on the Rio Grande a few days ago and had decided they would go ahead and kill all the white and Mexican men they came across. These three men happened along at the wrong time for them, but the right time for Nasay.

Nasay had seen twenty-eight winters. Being a great warrior, he was able to 'afford' to have the chief's daughter as his wife. They had a son and was happy for three winters...until the white man raided his ranchero while most of the warriors were away hunting. His wife and child were killed, as were most of the men's wives and children who rode with him. They rode not only with a hate for the whites invading their land but with extra hate for what they had done.

~~~

Yancy had slept till almost daylight. By the time he got Billy up and around, the eastern sky was turning gray.

"Gonna be a beautiful day, Billy."

"Shoulder feels better. Get a little more food in my belly and you're right, it's a good day," Billy said.

"WHAT THE HELL!" Yancy yelled as a multitude of shots could be heard, maybe a half mile or so away. He scrambled up the bank to take a look. Billy was right behind him.

"Sounds like a damn war," Billy said as more shots were heard. They could not see anything from where they were. "Wonder if it's the boys and that damn scout caught up with them?"

"Sounds to me there's too much shooting to be just seven or eight men," Yancy answered. "Let's see if we can find out without being seen." They started in the direction of the shots but staying as close as possible to the river so they could disappear down the bank if they had to.

~~~

"Oh GOD!" Curt had screamed pointing to the ridge behind them. Dale and Jake both looked where he was pointing. Ten or twelve Apaches were coming down the ridge toward them.

"MOUNT UP," Dale hollered. "Let's get the hell outa here." The three men were racing their horses away from the Apaches coming down the ridge. Four Apaches showed themselves to their right and the three men slightly changed their direction…right at the Apaches waiting in the draw. Dale and Jake had their repeaters out and were firing as fast as they could from the back of their horses.

"DAMN," Jake said as they all seen the Apaches rise up in front of them. Jake, in the lead, was knocked out of his saddle and cartwheeled backwards, dead before he hit the ground with three holes in his chest. Dale, hit in the shoulder and barely hanging onto his horse, led Curt up a slope to get to the high ground; Curt didn't make it, two bullets in the back ended his wish of getting back home for his birthday. He hit the ground hard and rolled over to look for Dale, expecting help. Dale never slowed down and lying low in the saddle, was doing his best to get away and not worrying about anyone else.

Curt had no feelings in his legs. He wanted to get into a position to defend himself but they would not move. He pulled his pistol and turned toward the on- coming Apaches…just in time to see a lance, thrown at close range, coming at his chest. The long point of the lance went deep into his chest. He grasped the shaft, trying to pull it out but it seemed he had no strength.

"MOTHER," he screamed as he saw the tomahawk arching thru the air at his head…then nothing.

Dale was just reaching the crest of the hill when his horse went down, his strength gone from the loss of blood from two bullets in his flanks. Dale hit hard and rolled, coming up on his feet. He whirled around toward the charging Apaches and brought his rifle up. It barked twice and the lead Apache left his horse, hitting the ground as limp as a rag doll. Dale was running toward some boulders when a bullet took his legs out from under him. He lost the rifle when he hit the ground. He started to get up but was knocked flat by an

Apache who had leaped from his horse onto Dale's back. The white man's struggle ended quickly with a knife stuck deep between the shoulder blades.

Nasay rode up and looked down at the dead white man, nodded toward the young Apache who had killed him, and turned his mount back down the hill. The young Apache scalped the man and with the bloody scalp in his raised fist screamed "AIYEEE, AIYEEE." The rest of the braves came to the body of Dale and with knives, took their hate out on it as they had the other two.

~~~

Tye had wanted to help the three even though they were sorry human beings, but he knew better. There were a lot of shots fired and then it was silent and he knew it was over for the three men. He would wait for awhile, bury the remains and then find the patrol. Once joined up with them, he felt confident they could handle twenty-five or so Apaches...with a little luck.

They waited thirty minutes before they walked their mounts out of the stand of mesquite they were in. Tye wanted to make sure the Apaches did not come their way. They did not go far before they found what they expected. The three men were shot and mutlilated beyond belief. Tye took a look around and came back to where Garrison and Christian were.

"We got a real problem, Lieutenant," Tye said as he dismounted.

Garrison, barely able to hold down what little he had on his stomach, looked toward him. "What problem besides these three men, the two that have escaped, and twenty-five Apaches that are close by?"

"These ain't a bunch of youngsters on the loose, but seasoned warriors, or at least some of them are."

"How do you know?"
~~~

"Youngsters, aching to prove themselves would have charged in an tried to just overrun the three men. They would have lost several men because they had no clue about the repeating rifles. These Apaches split their force and put several men there;" he pointed with his rifle to a small draw about thirty yards away. "They were there before daylight. The rest showed themselves on that ridge over there behind the three men. It was a good plan because the leader of that bunch knew the men whould mount their horses and flee the opposite direction…right into the men in the draw. They never had a chance. They got off a few shots but being accurate from a running horse is impossible. I doubt if the Apache lost a single man. Another thing that bothers me is the way the men were butchered. This is one upset bunch, Lieutenant."

~~~

Yancy and Billy were watching Tye and the rest from the top of a low hill about one hundred and fifty yards away. They had witnessed the bodies of their friends being dragged to a spot under a large cedar and buried. Yancy's insides were burning with hate for this damn scout and renewed his vow to kill him in the worst way he could.

"Guess they just ambushed them didn't they? Didn't give the boys a chance." Billy mumbled.

"Don't know and I don't care but that damn scout and the other two are going to pay for what they done to my boys," Yancy replied. "If I had my rifle instead of this damn single shot Spencer, they would right now," he added as the two of them scooted back down from the crest on their bellies aways before standing up and walking back to the river.

"What's the plan?" Billy asked as he scooped a handful of water from the river and took a drink.

"Horses, we have to get us some horses first, then some food and then more ammunition. There should be some more homesteaders along the river. We'll find one and
~~~

get what we need…maybe even a woman or two." He smiled, thinking of having a woman for awhile. "Yeah, that's all we need right now, horses, food, ammunition, and a woman…in that order."

They crawled to the top of the river bank and began walking southeast, never getting out of sight of the river and the safety of having it to their backs if trouble should come. They had no clue that the Apache killed their three friends, not Tye and his group. They were not looking for Apaches, just the cavalry and that damn scout.

Chapter Fifteen

"When are we gonna get after those two that got away...Yancy and Billy?" Christian asked.

Tye, his hands on the saddle pommel and standing in the stirrups to ease his butt some, answered after looking in all directions. "I want to find those two but right now we need to be concerned more with twenty-five or so Apaches that are loose. They can do a whole lot more damage than the Cates. I just hope the patrol is alert because they probably don't have a clue about the Apaches. They are looking for us or the gang that they don't know is already dead. I hope Dan August is scouting for them. He can probably keep them out of trouble."

Garrison, who had said nothing, just listening, suddenly pointed south, toward the river. "Smoke," he said. Tye and Christian both looked in that direction. As they looked the gray smoke increased and turned black.

"What is it?" Christian asked.

"Homestead," Tye answered as he sat back down in the saddle and headed in that direction. Garrison and Christian were bringing up the rear and trying to catch up. Tye pulled the brim of his hat down low to keep it on his head as he headed toward the homestead at a gallop. He gave Sandy his head, letting him pick the best path to run in. He glanced back and saw that Christian and Garrison were right behind him.

They had gone about two miles when Tye pulled up, just short of the top of a ridge. The smoke was thick just on the other side of the hill and one could smell the pungent odor of wood mixed with burnt flesh.

"Hold here while I take a look," Tye said as he dismounted and handing Sandy's reins to Christian. When he got close to the top, he took off his hat and dropped to his hands and knees, bear crawling to the top. Looking over the top thru some scrub-brush, he saw what he expected to see and a whole lot more. Several bodies were scattered around the front of the burning home and corral. Two more could be seen leaning up against the wood fence around the corral.

He looked around, farther away from the homestead, to make sure everything was okay and no one was nearby. From where he was, this massacre looked like it had happened not more than a hour ago. He stood up and motioned for the other two to come on up. When they arrived, he mounted Sandy and started down the slope toward the homestead...and a scene that Garrison and Christian would never forget.

As they entered the yard, two young men were lying close together butchered beyond belief: scalped, hands cut off and eyes dug out of their sockets. Two young boys, probably seven or eight years old were shot and other than scalped, not mutilated. Two women were spread eagle on the ground, stripped and surely raped over and over before their throats had been cut. Tied to the fence was the worse. Two older men, probably the husbands of the two women, were sitting on the ground, backs to the fence and arms tied around the poles. Tye looked at them and then at the women and swore.

"I told you this is a bad bunch, Lieutenant. They wounded these two and tied them so they would have to watch their women being raped. That had to be real torture for a man to see that but then the worse happened." Tye dismounted. "Take a look at this." Garrison and Christian dismounted and came to where Tye was. They both turned away at the sight that they had not noticed at first look. A fire had been placed and lit between the men's legs. Both Christian and Garrison shuddered at the thought of what pain that caused. "They probably passed out and then, before the Apaches left, they shot each of them in the right eye at close range. You never want to be captured alive by an Apache and I assure you, not by this bunch." He walked into the tool shed and came out with shovels. "Let's get the burying done and get out of here and make camp at least a couple miles away."

~~~

Five miles southeast of where Tye was, the patrol was making its way through the canyons, searching for signs of Tye, Garrison, and Christian.

The patrol, led by Captain McClellan had been moving fast since they had left the fort, taking only a few brief stops for the men to stretch their legs, answer nature's call, and water their mounts. They had covered about forty miles.

"I think it's about time to give the men and horses a good break, Captain. They are plum worn out. A good meal under their belts would make a world of difference. The way they are right now, they wouldn't be worth a plug nickel in a fight," Dan said. He was scouting for the patrol and was Tye's best scout so McClellan listened to him.

"Lieutenant Blanco, tell the men we are stopping for an hour or so. Take care of their mounts and make themselves a hot meal."

"Yes sir," Blanco said and turned to Sergeant Crowell, "You heard the Captain. Take care of it."

Crowell passed the word to the men. You could see the relief in the men's faces as they dismounted and took care of their mounts. A few minutes later, two small fires were going and the aroma of fresh coffee and fried bacon filled the air. The men were in a good mood after filling their bellies and lots of jokes filled the air.
~~~

"Sorta figured we would have found the patrol by now," McClellan said to his scout, August.

"Me too," Dan answered, "but knowing Tye the way I do, I figure he'll find us. He's like a damn Apache you know, you won't see him till he wants you too."

"From what Roberts told the major about this bunch they were after, I hope they are still on their feet."

"I'll tell you something, Captain, and it's not anything you don't already know. If the Apache can't corral him after all these years, I don't think some ex-confederate soldiers have a snowballs chance in hell of doing it. He's more Apache than an Apache is. While back, we were watching a large group of them at a Rancherio on the Rio Grande. We took turns watching. One morning, about two a.m., he was sleeping and when my watch was over I tried sneaking down and surprise him. Mind you, Captain, I ain't no tenderfoot and I can sneak up on anyone when I want to. Done it mor'n once to an Apache. That damn Tye woke up before I got within twenty foot of him. No sir, ain't no ex-soldiers gonna capture him."

"It will be dark in an hour, tell the men we will go ahead and make camp. Make sure Sergeant Crowell sets the sentries for the night." Blanco left to carry out his orders and the camp quickly settled in for the night. McClellan sat on his bedroll thinking about things…things in the past and things to come. He thought about Tye and what Dan had said about him. He had known other men like Tye. He chuckled to himself and mumbled; "That's crazy; there are no other men like Tye." He was sure Tye's father had been just like him, but no others. He was a career man and Clark was the third fort he had been assigned to. He had seen a dozen or so 'he's the best scout in the army,' in the last three years. Hell, there's not one of them that could even begin to compare to Watkins. He lay down and pulled the wool army issue blanket up to his chin. 'Nights are getting chilly,' he thought to himself and drifted off to sleep.

~~~

Nasay, on top of a ridge almost a quarter of a mile away, watched the patrol through the glasses that see far. He had picked the binoculars up at the last homestead they had raided. He was shocked at first when he looked through them. He was looking at a horse fifty yards away and he reached out his hand thinking he could touch the horse. Each man with him had to look through them and each was amazed.

He watched the soldiers making camp and noted where the guards were posted. He wasn't sure he wanted to attack them as of this moment. He would decide later, besides the sun was dropping behind the hills and he was, as most Apache were, against fighting at night. He looked at the scout through the glasses and was glad it was not the scout, Watkins. He knew Watkins by sight, having seen him once at a council between Juh-nah and an officer that was in charge. He could not remember the officer's name but all the Apache knew Watkins. He was a great warrior and his people believed him to be part Apache. The brave who killed him would be great medicine among his people. He knew many had tried, but all had failed.

He was glad that Watkins was not here because it would be easier to fool the soldiers without his being around. He wondered why this patrol was here and why so many soldiers. There was as many of them as he had men. He looked the camp over one more time and then backed down from the ridge and made his way to his men shouting orders to make camp by the river which was a mile to the southwest.

He sat on the bank of the river thinking of the past as he filled his gourd with water. Visions of his wife, his young son, and the happy life they had came to him. That was before the white soldiers came while most of the warriors were away hunting. Only old men, women, and children were in the camp when the soldiers came. A few escaped but most
~~~

were killed including his wife, child, and father. He and the men with him had vowed they would avenge the killing and would fight the white man for as long as blood flowed through their veins, such was their hate.

He knew the reputation of the scout, Watkins, as a man of his word. The Apache felt all white men spoke out of both sides of their mouths, but Watkins was like an Apache in that he always spoke the truth... from the heart. He had great respect for this man but would not hesitate to kill him if he had a chance. He stood up and walked back to camp trying to decide if he would attack the soldiers in the morning and if so, how would he do it.

~~~

Back at headquarters, Thurston was pacing the floor. The one thing he hated about his job was the waiting...waiting and nothing he could do about anything. He had visited the hospital and spoke with Roberts and Arnold. He was shocked at the story they told of just how bad this bunch was. He had been here at Clark for a year now, and his resolve to rid this country of scum like the Cates and the Apache was as strong now as it was then. The country was filling up with men and women trying to make a go of it in this land and by God, he was going to make it safe for them if it was the last thing he did.

A knock on his door ended his thoughts.

"Come!" he said.

The door opened and his aide, Corporal Henderson stepped in.

"Sir. Mr. McDovitt is requesting to see you."

"Send him in."

"Evening Majur," Buff said as he entered and shook Thurston's hand.

"Good evening to you, Buff. What do I owe this pleasure to?"
~~~

"Rebecca's bin havin' sum wurries abut wather Tye wus okay ar not."

"As far as I know he is just fine. I have sent Captain McClellan and a patrol to find them."

"Figgured as much. Tye's like his pappy, a hard man ta kill. Whut's tha situation?"

"There is Tye, Lieutenant Garrison, and Private Christian left and they are trying to do several things: finding the gang, controlling their prisoners, the Cates brothers, finding the patrol I sent to meet them, and trying to stay alive."

"Damn! I'm glad ta heer he ain't in no truble," Buff said smiling.

"Truth is, Buff, I think the situation they are in is a bad one. This bunch they are after is as bad as I have heard about. I know they will have their hands full just keeping those pieces of scum, the Cates, from escaping."

"This heer McClellan. He a gud man?"

Thurston laughed. "He is as good as I have and he will do whatever it takes to help Tye. He owes Tye."

"How's that?"

"He made a mistake a while back and got his men in an Apache ambush. Tye came in with some men and bailed him out. I don't want to lie to Rebecca and tell her everything is fine so just tell her this. Tye is alive and well at the last report. He should be meeting up with McClellan tonight or tomorrow. Maybe that will ease her worry some."

"Will do, Major. I'll chek with ya in tha morn'n ta see if'n enee news cums in."

Chapter Sixteen

The night passed quietly and dawn found the patrol heading northwest hoping to stumble onto Tye. Dan was out in front looking for any sign of the patrol. He was not aware of who was watching him from a ridge several hundred yards away. Nasay had decided not to attack the patrol but if they continued the way they were heading yesterday, he might just have a surprise for them. He had several men on both sides of the canyon he figured they would pass through. He also had some of his men in the canyon floor, in holes, covered with sand and almost invisible to anyone who was passing by. They would rise up among the soldiers and fire point blank into them.

Dan had passed three of the buried Apaches and was fifty yards into the canyon when he pulled up. Something was bothering him but he could not put his finger on what it was. He signaled McClellan to stop. The hair on the back of his neck was standing up like it always does when trouble was near. He looked at the canyon walls on both sides carefully, but saw nothing. He started walking his horse back out of the canyon being careful not to act like anything was wrong.

He even whistled some stupid song that he didn't know the name of.

Arriving back at the patrol, he relaxed and realized he was soaking wet from sweat and it was early morning and cool.

"What's the matter, Dan?" McClellan asked.

"Don't know, Captain. Just had me a feeling something was wrong."

"Wrong," McClellan repeated. "What do you mean, wrong?"

"Captain, men like me and Tye stay alive because we have an extra sense that most men don't have...a sense that warns us of trouble. I just got one of those feelings when I was in that canyon up there. Don't know for sure if anything is wrong or not. Didn't see anything, just that damn feeling."

"Do we have to go through the canyon or can we skirt it and go around?" McClellan asked.

"We could go around but it would cost us at least a half a day."

"What do you suggest then?"

"That canyon is only about a half mile long. A man on a running horse is not that easy to hit. I suggest we hit it at full speed and have the men lay low in the saddle."

McClellan mulled the suggestion over in his head and at the same time, searched for another alternative. He made one mistake and it could have cost his and his men's lives, and would have if not for Tye. He did not want a blemish of losing a lot of men in an ambush on his record. Then, he remembered what Tye told him after Tye pulled he and his men from certain death. "You can't let getting tricked by the Apache affect the way you do things in the future. Don't be afraid of making mistakes, we all do. Sometimes you have to throw away the book and go with what your gut feeling tells you to do." This, McClellan figured may be one of those times.

He took another look at the canyon and then the surrounding area. He did not think it would be the thing to do to go around. His orders were specific. Find the men left from the patrol as quickly as possible and bring the scum in they were chasing. He figured he had no other choice.

"LIEUTENANT BLANCO," he hollered.

"SIR," Blanco said as he rode up to McClellan and Dan.

"We are going to hit that canyon full speed. Dan thinks there is a problem there, maybe the gang we are looking for expecting to ambush us.

Have the men take out their pistols, and when we hit the canyon opening, lay as low in the saddle as they can. Understood?"

"Yes Sir." Blanco turned and rode back to the men to convey the orders.

~~~

Nasay was curious as to what was going on with the patrol. Did the scout see something? He glanced around and could not see the hidden men so he didn't think the scout saw anything either. But why are they not coming? What is the scout telling the leader of the patrol? He was relieved a moment later when he saw the soldiers start forward at a fast trot.

Nasay and his close friends, Calita and Cato, had the rifles that never run out of bullets they took from the three men they killed yesterday. It took them a while to figure out how they worked but the Apache were good at solving problems. Nasay and Cato were side by side on the right side of the canyon. Calito was on the other side. About half of Nasay's men had the single shot Sharps, the rest had bows. At close range like this would be, the bows were deadly. The Apache could shoot their arrows accurately and could release several of them in less than a minute. He looked back at the patrol. In a few seconds they would be in his trap.

~~~

Tye, Garrison, and Christian were about a mile west of the canyon. Tye figured they should be running into the patrol this morning and they had been moving at a fast pace, looking for any sign of them. They were spread out looking for tracks in case they had missed them. The only tracks they had found so far were unshod...Apache ponies. Tye had one eye on the ground and the other looking for trouble.

He pulled Sandy up and hollered at the other two. “LIEUTENANT, CHRISTIAN.” When they looked at him he raised his hand and rotated it in a circular motion. They knew the assembly signal and came fast to where Tye was.

“There’s a canyon ahead that the patrol is going to have to come through. I don’t think they have yet or we would have seen some sign. We are not too far behind the Apache whose tracks I’m sure you have seen so be...,” he didn’t finish as gunfire came from the direction of the canyon.

~~~

Nasay was shocked when the soldiers began racing their horses into the canyon. He fired and that was the signal for the rest to open up. A deadly barrage of bullets and arrows fell on the soldiers.

“WHAT THE HELL!” McClellan shouted. “WHERE IN HELL’S NAME DID THESE APACHES COME FROM?” Behind him, horses were going down and men were screaming as the bullets and arrows found some of them.

“SONOFABITCH!” Dan screamed when he saw the rope stretched across their path. He saw it to late and his horse went down as did McClellan’s. The charging horses, eyes bulging with all that was going on, piled into the horses that were down. The men hit the ground hard, some were knocked unconscious, others stunned momentarily. Dan ran behind some large rocks, holding his busted shoulder. McClellan was close behind him with only bumps and a cut on his forehead. Blanco was dead, two arrows prodruding from his back. Several horses were down, others milled about. Troopers were dragging the wounded to the cover of the rocks. When the dust settled, McClellan could see several of his men behind the rocks. He also saw several scattered along the floor of the canyon, obviously dead.

“Where did the Apaches come from?” McClellan asked.
~~~

"Not sure," Dan answered. "Didn't know any were in the area and we have had no reports of a renegade band. Like I told you before, Tye and me saw a couple hundred a few days ago at a camp on the Rio Grande. Several different tribes of Apache were there. They dispersed and we thought all of them went back to their homelands. We've had no reports of hostilities."

"Well, we sure as hell found some hostiles," McClellan said firing his pistol. An Apache who exposed himself a second too long tumbled down the side of the canyon.

"We are in a hell of a fix, Captain. It won't be long before they charge up the canyon. They will leave a few in the rocks firing to keep our heads down and they will over run us. In hand to hand fighting, the men won't have a chance against them."

"We need to get the men together. We'll stand a better chance that way than scattered the way we are now."

"Good idea, Captain." Dan was looking for a better place than where they were and he found it only twenty yards away. A boulder, the size of a house had toppled from the side of the canyon leaving a huge depression in the wall of the canyon. It would give them protection from both sides and offer a good field of fire up the canyon if the Apache should charge them.

"SERGEANT CROWELL!" McClellan shouted.

"CROWELL IS DOWN, SIR," a trooper answered.

"Damn," McClellan muttered. "CORPORAL PHIPPS."

"YO," Phipps replied.

McClellan waited a second before giving his orders. "Phipps, do you see that depression of the side of the canyon where that boulder fell?"

Phipps looked and spotted the place McClellan was talking about. "YES, SIR. I SEE IT."

"Make sure all of your men can see it. When I give the word, all of you make a break for it. Help the wounded and if any of you can, grab a canteen from the horses that are down. We'll need it. Are you ready?"

Phipps looked around at the men before answering. He told them when the Captain yelled, run like hell and don't run in a straight line, and don't stop except to try and grab the canteens. He turned back toward the Captain's location. "YES, SIR."

"NOW," McClellan shouted as he and Dan broke for the depression. The Apaches were frantically firing as fast as they could. Fortunatley, most were not that good of marksman with a rifle but a few were and one could hear the 'thunk' of bullets hitting flesh. The ones with the bows were doing the most damage. They were firing as fast as they could notch an arrow and the air was full of the deadly, feathered darts. Six more men were down but the rest scrambled into the depression. One man was still coming, a private Madison, and he was running like the devil was after him while carrying five or six canteens that he had stopped to pickup. Ten yards from the depression, he was hit in the back and a bloody flint point protruded from his chest. He fell, lay there a couple of seconds, then struggled to his feet and was almost to where the men waited when a bullet struck him again in the back, knocking him down. He was five feet from where McClellan was. He looked McClellan in the eyes and with the last of his strength, tossed the canteens into the depression...and died.

McClellan, shocked at the man's death so close to the safety of the depression, stared at the man. "What's that man's name, Phipps?"

"Madison, Sir. Private Bob Madison."

"I'll remember," McClellan mumbled still looking at the man. "I'll remember," he repeated.

~~~

"What do you think, Tye?" Garrison asked.
~~~

"Patrol has got themselves ambushed."

"What are we going to do?"

"There's three of us. What do you think we can do, charge in and scare the hell out of the Apaches?" Tye said angrily. He saw Garrison's shock at the harsh words. "Sorry that came out the way it did, Lieutenant. The frustration of the situation, I guess. We'll figure something out." He looked around and saw the bugle on Christian's saddle

"You might have just saved the day, private. Can you play that?" pointing to the bugle.

"Some…okay, I guess."

"What do you have in mind, Tye?" Garrison asked.

"What if we tie some mesquite to our horses and drag them behind us raising a hell of a dust storm,and at the same time, Christian here blows the bugle call for charge. The Apaches will see us and a lot of dust and think there's a larger number than three."

"Do you think it will work?"

"Probably not," Tye said smiling, "but do you have a better idea. Besides, if it don't, the Apache has a great saying for situations like this."

"What's that?"

"It's a good day to die." Tye dismounted and with his Bowie, begin cutting large branches from the mesquites. Garrison sat on his horse trying to figure out the meaning of what Tye just said.

Christian mumbled… "A good day to die? It ain't ever a good day to die."

"Throw me some rope," Tye hollered. He tied several branches behind each horse. "Let's move in closer to the canyon."

~~~

Every time McClellan or one of the men raised their heads, a barrage of bullets came their way. It was as the
~~~

scout said; they will keep our heads down and then will be on top of us with knives and tomahawks.

"Check your pistols and make sure they are loaded. They will be on us anytime. Fire as fast as you can and then use your sabers. Good luck men." McClellan tuned back to face what he knew was coming, figuring he had issued his last command.

"HERE THEY COME!" Dan yelled. From the sound of the Apaches screams, one might think the whole Apache nation was coming. It scared the hell out of every man, but they were soldiers, and most had seen this before. They were ready and when the first wave of Apaches reached the top of the depression, the rifle fire from them riddled every Apache that came over. The second wave was right behind the first and some made it into the depression, swinging their knives and tomahawks. The troopers, desperation showing in every face, fought like madmen, swinging their sabers. The sound of tomahawks cracking skulls, the noise of the pistols, and screams of pain mixed with the Apache yells was deafening. McClellan had his saber stuck through the stomach of an Apache that had just split a trooper's head open with his tomahawk. Dan, unable to fight except with his pistol because of his busted shoulder, had his back against the wall of the depression firing his pistol. Phipps had shot one and was wrestling with another doing his best to keep from getting his head split open. The Apache broke away and took a wild swing that Phipps ducked and struck upward with his saber. The bloody point was sticking a foot out of the back of the brave. The Apache stood like a statue even after Phipps pulled the blade out. Phipps looked into the Apache's dead eyes, then with his hand, pushed him and he fell backwards, onto a large flat rock. Suddenly it was over. The Apache pulled back leaving a scene that McClellan had seen before and hoped to never see again. Bodies, both troopers and Apaches, covered the bottom of the depression. Some places had bodies stacked two and three high. It was suddenly very quiet. The only noise was the moaning of the wounded.

"Use your damn sabers and make sure there are no Apaches left alive," McClellan commanded. "PHIPPS!"

Phipps came to where McClellan was. "Yes Sir."

"Get me a casualty report."

"Yes, Sir. Be right back Sir."

"ARROWS COMING IN!" an excited trooper yelled. All heads turned to the sky and suddenly it was a mad house, men scrambling to find cover. Fortunately, the arrows fell just short with only a couple finding the depression, sticking harmlessly in the rocky ground.

"The next bunch will be dead on Captain. You had better find some cover," Dan stated.

"What cover?" McClellan asked.

"QUITE," Dan hollered. "LISTEN." The unmistakable sound of a bugle sounding charge could be heard in the distance. The sound of running horses could be heard also.

"THEY ARE PULLING OUT, SIR. THE APACHES ARE LEAVING." Phipps hollered as other troopers begin to realize what was happening and were as excited as Phipps. They came out of the depression and looked toward the far end of the canyon where the sound of the bugle came from. They could see some men and a lot of dust. "What do you make of it, Dan?"

Dan with eyes as sharp as any Apache started laughing. "It's Tye and the others. I'd recognize Tye's horse, Sandy, anywhere."

"Where did the others come from? The major said there were only three men left of the patrol."

Dan laughed again. "I'll be a sonofabitch. That beats all I ever saw."

"What in the devil are you talking about?"

"Those 'other' men you see is brush being pulled behind the horses raising dust to make it look like a patrol."

One of the men took the pole the company banner was on and began waving it to get the riders attention. In a few seconds, the three rode up to where the grateful men were. Christian was off his horse immediately and was with his fellow troopers, shaking hands, and slapping backs.

With the men gathered around, McClellan spoke up. "This is the second time you saved mine and my men's butts, Tye. I'm…no we, are very grateful."

"Well this time you can thank Christian there. We could not have pulled that stunt off if he hadn't picked up that bugle." All eyes went to Christian who was soaking up the attention. He took off his hat and with a sweeping motion brought it across in front while bowing. "Your welcome," he said laughing as the men gathered around him, patting him on the back again.

Phipps approached MCClellan with the casualty report. "Eleven dead, four wounded, Sir. Two of the wounded are able to keep going and two need medical attention which we can't give here."

"Very well. Thank you, Corporal." He turned to Tye and Garrison as the men were stacking the dead Apaches. "I'm going to have to send a man back with the dead and wounded if we continue the patrol. That leaves me with eight men counting myself."

"If I may suggest, Sir," Tye said. "Let's spread out and make a sweep back where we came from toward the Pecos and see if we can find any tracks of the Cates. There's a total of eleven of us. We can spread out and cover a lot of ground." He then explained how the Cates escaped.

"How long will it take?" McClellan asked. I hate leaving the wounded and dead here for long."

"Maybe, two or three hours."

"Do you think the Apaches are gone? I'd hate to think about them coming back and attack the wounded men."

"They're gone, Captain," Tye replied. Apaches are great fighters but they aren't dumb. They believe a patrol came in to rescue you. They think they are outnumbered now. They may come for their dead later, so let's take our wounded and dead with us for a mile or so and then leave them."

"Let's get it done, then. PRIVATE MASON," he hollered.

"Yes, Sir." Mason answered.

"We are going about a mile or so toward the Pecos. We will leave the dead and wounded there while we see if we can find the Cates. You will stay there with the wounded and the dead. We will be back in no more than three hours."

"Yes Sir."

Chapter Seventeen

Leaving the dead and the wounded behind, Garrison had the men spread out about a hundred yards apart, looking for any footprints. They were spread from the bank of the Rio Grande to over a quarter mile away from it. Tye, Garrison, and McClellan were in the middle with Phipps on one end and Christian on the other, walking the bank.

They had been moving for almost an hour when Christian shouted he found tracks. He waited for Tye and the officers to come. He didn't want to mess up by adding more tracks. Arriving quickly, Tye dropped to one knee, reading the tracks. He followed them for a hundred yards before saying anything.

"We're on top of them, Captain," Tye said speaking softly. "These tracks are only minutes old, thirty at the most. I think they are just below us, hiding along the bank."

They walked back away from the bank to talk. The men gathered around them. "Men, Tye thinks the men we are looking for are close, hiding along the bank. I want you to approach the bank about twenty yards apart. Be ready because these two are not likely to surrender knowing they are going to hang. Now, move out."

With the men spread on each side of them, Tye stood on top of the bank.

"YANCY!" he yelled. "YOU AND BILLY MIGHT AS WELL COME OUT AND GIVE YOURSELVES UP. THERE ARE A DOZEN MEN UP HERE."

"What are we gonna do, Yancy," Billy whispered.

"I'll tell you one thing we're not gonna do and that's give up. I'd rather die here with a bullet than wait for a hanging."

Yancy put his hand on Billy's shoulder and looking him in the eyes, nodded. Billy nodded back and they sprang out of their hiding place with Billy firing his rifle and Yancy, his revolver. They hit no one but both were hit several times by the soldiers. Billy was dead before he crumpled to the ground; Yancy staggard backwards and fell into the water. Tye jumped down to the water's edge, grabbed Yancy by the collar and pulled him out. Quickly studying his wounds, Tye slapped him on the face, bringing Yancy around. "You ain't gonna die from these wounds, but I'll promise you one thing you murdering bastard, you will hang from the gallows in Brackett." Yancy tried to say something but Tye knocked him cold with a hard right.

"This one's dead, Sir," Phipps said looking at McClellan. "Yancy will live to hang," Tye added.

"Get Yancy up here so we can look at his wounds," McClellan ordered. With Yancy stretched out on the ground, McClellan inspected his wounds. One bullet hit him in the upper thigh and one high on the left side of his chest. Tye rolled him on his side and saw the exit holes. "Went clean through, Captain." He'll be hurting some but that will be good for him." Regardless of what had happened, some of the men laughed at the remark. McClellan ordered a man to patch and bind the wounds and then had Tye make a travois so they could get him back to Fort Clark. Dan walked up to Tye.

"Been intending to ask you, where in the hell did those Apaches come from?"

"Been thinking about that since we came across them yesterday. I think maybe they are some of the ones we saw at the rancherio the other day. Maybe they just wanted to hang around and see if they could cause some trouble. I'll tell you one thing, they are an older, experienced bunch and one more thing, they are about as angry as any I have ever seen."

"How's that?"

"You should have seen what they did to some homesteaders and three of the guys we were looking for. Never saw anyone butchered like they were." They mounted their horses and Tye turned back to Dan. "By the way, how's the shoulder?"

"Feels great...as long as I don't move or breathe." Dan said grimacing as his horse took its first step... "It's gonna be a long ride back to the fort."

~~~

Nasay sat under a mesquite, away from his men. He was furious at the way his ambush had worked out. He wondered where the other soldiers came from. He had come from where the troopers had come. How did he or any of his men not see them? From the amount of dust, they had to be many of them. He thought about the dust for a moment. Was there too much dust? The ground was pretty hard and rocky and he had noticed his men had not raised as much dust as the soldiers had.

He stood up and hollered at one of his braves, his good friend, Tashay.

Tashay came over to him. "What does my friend want?" he asked.

"Walk with me," Nasay answered. "I have been thinking about the soldiers that came. I don't think there was very many. I think we were tricked by the white eyes."

"Why do you think this? You saw the dust and heard their horn."

"There was too much dust, Tashay. I would like you to backtrack and see if you can find them. Take two men and enough ponies to bring our dead back."

Tashay nodded his understanding and turned to leave.
~~~

"Be careful my friend. Do not get into a fight with the soldiers." He handed his friend the glasses that see far. "Take these. They will help you see."

~~~

The patrol had picked up the wounded and the dead troopers and was making its way back to the fort. Tye figured after the last three days, they could all use a little rest. Dan's shouder was hurting him something fierce so a travois was made for him also. The travois was simple to make and was fairly comfortable for an injured man. The Indians had used it for no telling how many years to haul supplies. It was simply two poles with a blanket stretched between and one end of the poles tied to opposite sides of the saddle, with the other ends dragging on the ground behind the horse.

Tye was out in front but only a couple hundred yards instead of his usual quarter of a mile or so. He wasn't expecting trouble but a man stays alive out here by always being ready if it came. They had passed where the ambush had taken place and like he figured, the dead Apaches were gone. These Apaches bothered him…more than most others he had fought. The way the ambush was set up, especially the rawhide ropes stretched across the path the troopers would go told him that this was a dangerous, smart, and highly upset bunch. He wasn't sure how many exactly there were, but from looking at the tracks earlier, he figured about twenty or so. Not a lot but then again, with the Apache, enough to be very concerned with, especially since they had only eleven troopers that could fight.

He smiled remembering Yancy regaining consciousness and smarting off about the stinking bluecoats. Christian smacked him good with the back of his hand. Yancy hadn't said a word since as far as he knew. He reined Sandy up to wait on the others to catch up. He rolled a smoke and after lighting it, looked around at the surrounding country side.
~~~

There had been an abundance of rain lately and everything was green except the purple sage that was blooming and was light purple, or pink to some people. Whatever the color, it was pretty.

~~~

Two hundred yards ahead and lying behind some of the purple sage, Tashay watched Tye through the binoculars. He knew this was the scout, Watkins because of the description Nasay had spoke of. He also saw that the soldiers numbered no more than the fingers on both his hands. He backed down the hill he was on and mounted his pony, anxious to get the news to Nasay that he had been right. They had been tricked by this scout.

~~~

"Is there a problem, Tye?" McClellan asked when he and the patrol arrived where Tye was.

"Not that I know of, Captain. Just sitting here, thinking about those Apaches. From the dead ones I saw, they were Mescalero. I told you Dan and me seen several groups of them at the rancherio the other day. It makes me wonder if there aren't other groups still hanging around to cause some trouble."

"I just hope this bunch has left and went back to their homes."

"I think they are still around. From what I have seen they are too damn mad to leave without killing a few more of us. You should have seen how they butchered those three men. That was not ritual mutilation, Sir that was mutilation for a whole different reason...pure hate."

"I've always wondered about the Apache and why they mutilated their victims," McClellan asked. "Why do they do that?"

Tye stood up in the stirrups and looked off in the distance, eastward. He thought he saw a little dust, but decided it was nothing. "To answer your question, Captain, the Apaches are like most other tribes. Whether it's the Kiowa, Comanche, Sioux, or Pawnee, they all believe that a man goes to the hereafter just like they left. In other words, they do not want an enemy to go for example, with both hands. So they cut off one or both. They might cut out their eyes even. They just don't want to meet their enemies in the hereafter and they be as healthy as they are."

"They believe in life after death?"

"Sure they do. Not in the same way we do, but they believe."

"I never would have guessed it."

"I'm gonna tell you something else, Captain. As far as being good people as a whole, they are probably better than the white man."

McClellan did a double take. "What do you mean by that?"

"They are all very loving parents to their children. Even the most vicious warrior is gentle to them. An Apache woman is risking her life if she commits adultery. They do not steal from one another and they don't lie."

"I see what you mean. That description would eliminate most white men in one way or another."

Dan, who had gotten painfully up off the travois, walked up to them just as Tye was speaking about the tracks he found.

"Another reason I think they are going to hang around is over there," Tye said pointing to some rocks slabs."

"That what I think it is?" Dan asked.

Tye nodded his head. "Yep."

"Damn," Dan said.

"What are you two talking about?" McClellan asked.

"They didn't take their dead with them, Sir. They buried them in shallow graves which mean they are not going home but staying," Dan said.

"Staying to see if they can kill some more of us," Tye said.

"Damn," McClellan muttered causing Dan and Tye to look at each other and smile. McClellan hardly ever cursed.

A low rumble from the southwest made them both look that direction. "Been watching that cloud for awhile; it's coming right at us and in a hurry." Tye looked at the canyon rim. "I suggest we get the men and horses up there," Tye said nodding upward. We're gonna get a little wet but up there, we should miss most of the wind." McClellan, looking at the rim told his sergeant to have the men dismount and lead their horses up the slope as it was to steep to risk injuring a horse.

~~~

Nasay was elated at the news Tashay brought. Not only was he right about the number of soldiers but Watkins was an extra gift. It would give him great satisfaction to kill the soldiers but to kill Watkins would make him known to all Apaches. He knew the stories of the other great warriors who had tried to kill this scout and failed. He knew they, like him, hated this man but respected him at the same time. There would be nothing but respect for Watkins when he was dead and his body would not be mutilated...the sign of respect by the Apache for a great warrior.

"Sit with me," Nasay said to Tashay. They walked to the shade of a large mesquite and sat down. "We need to plan how we are going to kill these soldiers. Tell me again about these soldiers."

"There are no more than twice the number of fingers on one hand. They have several that are dead tied to their ponies and have three on travois's that are wounded. They are maybe one hour behind me."
~~~

Nasay's said nothing but his mind was working fast, trying to come up with a plan. He stood up as did Tashay. "Since we are not familiar with this land, get the others and we will ride and see if we can find a place to surprise these white men. Have a couple cut branches and wipe out our tracks. We will make it difficult for Watkins to follow us... as will the rain." He nodded toward the ominious looking black cloud coming toward them.

~~~

The troopers were all huddled against the cliff wall. The horses were picketed and three soldiers were assigned to make sure they did not get away if they got too excited when the storm hit and break the picket line. The thunder was loud now and the lightning was flashing everywhere. The wind had a chill to it, suggesting the storm may have some hail in it. The men could see the gray wall of rain as it moved swiftly toward them. It was going to be one of those typical Texas storms. It will come in fast and furious and then be gone just as quick. They had all seen it before and knew what to expect.

When the storm hit, the rain was coming down in sheets and the wind was blowing it almost sideways. The men were protected pretty well from the main force of the storm but they were all getting soaked, even though they had their slickers on.

For the few minutes it took the storm to move on, it was hell on earth. Wind, lightning, thunder, and blinding rain made the men wish they could find a hole to crawl into. After it passed, the air smelled fresh, the landscape was greener with all the dust washed off the plants...and any tracks the Apaches might have left were gone. The men walked and slide their mounts down the muddy slope to the canyon floor and remounted them and when they were ready, McClellan gave the orders to move out. Tye was already out front by the
~~~

time the order to mount up was given. A wet and chilled group headed out.

Tye had been down this road before, knowing Apaches were near and no tracks to help him figure where they were. Situations like this made him feel alive. It heightened his senses, knowing any second could be his last on earth. He loved this job.

~~~

Nasay watched through the glasses that see far and confirmed what Tashay had said. It was Watkins leading the patrol and it was Watkins who had fooled them with the bugle. He hated this man who had done so much damage to his people but at the same time felt remorse at the thought that he would have to kill him. Watkins was probably the only white man who could be trusted and who understood the Apache. Nasay thought back to the first time he heard the name Watkins. He was young then and it was Tye's father, not Tye, who had the respect of the Apache. He was 'big medicine' to the Apache people and maybe even a little feared. One would never get an Apache to admit that for everyone knows, the Apache was known to fear no one.

He had found the place he would trap the soldiers. He had his braves dig the ground out around some huge rocks that were high on a cliff that overlooked the entrance to a canyon the soldiers would have to go through. By not going through this canyon he found they would have to travel way out of the way to get to the fort where he figured they were heading. He felt good about things as he scrambled from the rocks where he had been watching.
~~~

Chapter Eighteen

Tye, sitting on Sandy, was studying the canyon ahead of him and waiting on the patrol. He took the makings out and rolled himself a smoke. McClellan arrived just as he took his first drag on the cigarette. McClellan looked at the canyon entrance.

"What are you thinking?" he asked Tye.

"I think we are looking at trouble up there in that canyon; if I was looking for a place to ambush some soldiers; that would be it."

"Can we go around?"

Tye flicked the cigarette away. "Yes Sir, we could but we have a couple of wounded men that need help soon or they ain't gonna make it. Going around this canyon will probably add almost a day in getting that help."

"What do you suggest then?"

"Let me go in and look around first."

"Okay. Let me know when you want us to come in."

He walked Sandy slowly into the canyon, watching the rocks for any sign of the Apaches and at the same time, watching Sandy. Horses can hear and smell better than a human and Sandy has saved Tye's bacon a couple of times by warning him of trouble by a snort or a flick of the ears. He pulled sany up a few yards inside od the entrance of the canyon. He studied every inch of the walls, looking for signs. He knew trouble was here, he could feel it but he could not see it. Turning Sandy around, he walked him back out of the canyon and up to the men and McCellan.

"I think we are in for a fight, Sir. The choice is yours whether we go in or around. If you want to go in I suggest you put the wounded on a horse and tie them to a healthy man to keep him from falling off in case we have to make a run for it."

McClellan sat on his horse weighing the options...which was only two. He could ride around the canyon and probably see the two wounded men die, or go through the canyon, the shortest route to the fort. If the Apaches were there, more men could die. 'A hell of a decision to make,' he thought to himself. Tye had seen no sign of Apache but as Tye told him before, that don't mean they are not there. He thought for a few more seconds before making his decision.

"Let's make a run through the canyon," he said. "Sergeant, have the wounded tied to a man so they will not fall off. Have three others bring the wounded's horses."

In a couple minutes, the sergeant reported all was ready.

"Let's do it," Tye said.

As they entered the canyon, Tye and every man's eyes were searching the rocky wall of both sides of the canyon. Just as the last man got through the entrance, huge rocks began tumbling down toward the narrow entrance.

"Dammitt," Tye hollered. "We've got to get thru this canyon." He kicked Sandy in the flanks and was at top speed in a couple strides. Sandy didn't need any urging as he was at an all out run, sensing the urgency in his master's voice. Glancing back, Tye saw McClellan and the patrol right on his heels. As he turned back in the saddle, the rocks on both sides of the canyon erupted with rifle fire and with arrows whistling thru the air.

"FOLLOW ME," McClellan shouted and took off with his horse at a dead run with the others right on his horse's tail. They had run about two hundred yards when Tye, out in front, sat Sandy down on his haunches, sliding to a stop. McClellan and the others slide in behind him.

"DAMMIT TO HELL," Tye muttered loudly. A large group of Apaches were on the ground at the other end of the canyon. They had their rifles and bows ready to riddle the charging soldiers.

"TO THE ROCKS," Tye hollered as he whirled Sandy to the left, toward the canyon wall and the hope of finding safety for the men among the large rocks that were scattered along the steep wall of the canyon. He didn't have to say it twice as the men were hot on his heels. He cursed himself for being so damn stupid. In the rocks they dismounted and the troopers surrounded Tye and McClellan.

"SERGEANT," McClellan shouted.

"Here, Sir,"

"Take control of the water. Let each man have a swallow now and give you their canteens. You assign a man to make sure no one drinks until I say so."

"Yes Sir," the sergeant said and started shouting orders.

McClellan took off his hat and wiped his forehead with his sleeve. "What do you think, Tye?"

"I cannot believe I did not see that coming," Tye said dejectedly. "I knew they were there I just could not see any sign."

"You told me you thought they were there. It was my call," McClellan said dropping to a knee as a bullet whistled harmlessly over head. "YOU MEN GET YOURSELVES AND YOUR HORSES BEHIND THE ROCKS AND OUT OF SIGHT," he shouted. More bullets came in, ricocheting off the rocks above their heads. "KEEP YOUR HEADS DOWN."

Tye looked at some of the men's faces and felt better. These were good men. None showed the fear that had to be inside them. They would stand their ground.

"The Apache will not attack, Captain. They have us bottled up and we ain't going anywhere and they know it unless we make a break for the end of the canyon. We would lose some men for sure that way."

"What do you think our best chance would be?" McClellan asked.

Tye looked at the sun dropping behind the rim of the canyon. "Be dark pretty soon. Maybe we can do something then," Tye said. "Till then, we might as well make ourselves comfortable." To McClellan's amazement, he watched Tye lean back against a rock, and pull his hat down over his eyes. Tye wasn't going to sleep but wanted it quite so he could think things out. He was still mad at himself; he knew that sooner or later he would get a patrol ambushed. It had taken two years for it to happen which took in a lot of patrols. He figured the odds just caught up with him. He now had to figure a way for these men, who were depending on him, to get out of this mess.

~~~

Nasay was excited. The first part of his plan worked as planned and he had out smarted the great scout. The patrol was going no where unless they wanted to take a chance on losing a lot of men by charging out of the canyon. It would be dark soon and he knew the troopers would get ready for some rest. He had plans for them that would prevent them from getting much sleep.

Tashay approached him smiling broadly. "The presents for the white eyes are ready," he said. "When do you want to give them?"

Nasay smiled at his friend. "As soon as it is dark."

~~~

"You had better get a man or two to watch the slope behind us, Captain. Wouldn't want a surprise," Tye said.

"I thought you said the Apache wouldn't fight at night."

"They won't normally, unless they are sure they will not go to the 'happy hunting ground'."

Sentries were posted with changes every two hours. It was now almost full dark. Tye stood up and stretched. "Captain, let's have a talk." They walked to an area away from the men. "I think we may have a way out of here."

"Fire away, Tye. I sure don't have a clue on how to without losing a lot of men. I know we could bust out of here in the dark but that would be taking chances of not only getting shot but the horses stepping in holes and throwing men who would then be captured and tortured."

"Going cross country and not down to the Mail Road and following it to the fort, I figure will save ten or twelve miles. I don't think it's more than twenty miles in a straight line to the fort."

"What are you getting at?"

"Me sneaking out of here and heading cross country."

"On foot?" McClellan asked, astonished at such a thought.

"I can run about as good as any Apache, Sir. I figure I can trot about four or five miles and then walk till I get my wind back and go another four or so. I figure I can reach the fort by daylight and get a patrol here before dark tomorrow."

"I don't know, Tye. That sounds like it's stretching things some."

"It's the only thing I can come up with. I really"...he didn't finish

"WHAT THE HELL?" Hollered one trooper.

"LOOK OUT," screamed another.

"SWEET JESUS...THEY ARE THROWING RATTLESNAKES AT US," yelled the sergeant. Four or five rattlesnakes were among the rocks where the men were. Tye and Dan ran to them.

"JUST STAND STILL," Tye ordered all of them. He reached down and grabbed one by the tail and swinging it around his head threw it out of the rocks to the floor of the canyon. He grabbed another as did Dan and repeated the throw. Another snake was thrown in by the Apaches, almost hitting Dan.

"SONOFABITCH," Dan hollered, and reaching down, grabbed the snake and threw him away from the men. About that time, shots were fired by the Apaches, startling the shaken men.

"It's gonna be this way all night, Tye," Dan said.

"Yeah. They ain't gonna let us get any sleep."

"About what you said earlier, Tye. Do you think it will work?" McClellan asked.

"I think I can be back before dark tomorrow."

"Do it then." McClellan ordered.

"Listen to Dan, Sir. He knows the Apache as well as me." McClellan nodded his head.

"When are you leaving?"

"Let's explain to the men and I'll be leaving."

McClellan gathered all the men around him except the ones on sentry duty. "Tye is going to try to sneak out of here and get help. He thinks he can be back here before sundown tomorrow. It will be up to us to hold out till then. Any questions?" No one said anything but Tye could tell by the look on their faces there was some doubt.

"Listen men," Tye Said. "The Apache will try to play with your head some. They will probably throw another snake or so, fire some more shots, and every once in a while, cut loose with a scream. They want to keep you awake. A tired man can't fight as well as a rested one. I suggest you pair up in the rocks and one try to sleep while the other watches. I'll see you tomorrow." He took one canteen and slipped back into the rocks to work his way up the cliff.

He did not figure on more than two, at the most three, Apaches on this side. They were there to sound the alarm if any soldiers tried to escape over the rim. Working his way slowly up the slope he was searching for them as well as making sure he didn't dislodge any loose rocks. He was again thankful he wore the moccasin boots instead of the hard soled army issue boots. He looked back down toward the soldiers but it was too dark to see anything. Suddenly he froze like a statue, holding his breath. A rock moved just to his left. He slowly turned his head that way but could not see more than three feet. It would be that way until the moon come up which was only thirty or so minutes away. He had to be past the Apaches before then if he wanted to get away.

His ears strained for any sound and almost jumped out of his skin when loud laughter came from where he heard the rock.

"SNAKE," he heard one of the troopers scream followed by more laughter from the Apache. 'At least I know where one is,' Tye thought to himself. The other should be close he figured. 'At least I hope there is only two,' he muttered to himself. He climbed the last few feet and eased over the rim and then froze again. Another Apache was squatted beside a small fire about twenty feet away. Tye noticed the canvas bag lying beside the Apache and he could see movement from within the bag.

The Apache appeared to be dozing so Tye eased on over and made his way into the brush. He started to leave but an idea popped into his head...an idea so crazy it might just work. He circled to his right and made his way ever so quietly to just behind the dozing Apache. Tye held his pistol in his left hand so he could knock the Apache out if he woke up and reaching with his right hand, picked up the bag. The Apache hadn't moved. Tye untied the leather string on the bag and lay it back down beside the Apache. He eased back into the brush and waited. He didn't have to wait long.

The Apache screamed, "AIEEE," as a snake that had come out of the bag bit him on the thigh as he sat there. The other Apache came scrambling over the rim to see what the problem was. While he was busy catching the snakes and putting them back in the bag, cutting the man's thigh and bleeding the bite, Tye made good his escape.

He was a half mile away by the time the moon lite up the landscape. It was a beautiful night and one could see aways with the moon as bright as it was. After getting his bearings, he began running with the easy gait of the Apache, the miles passing quickly under his feet. He had run probably four miles before he had to change direction because of a canyon. He walked for thirty minutes, took a small drink, and began running again. He alternated running and resting the rest of the night. Dawn found him only about five miles from Clark. He was exhausted and knew the last five would be the worse. He drank the last of his water and walked a few more minutes. "Gonna have to get some more moccasins after this," he said outloud looking down at his torn boots. He began jogging the last leg of his trip.

~~~

The rim of the canyon opposite the patrol was was just beginning to receive the first rays of the rising sun, leaving the slope still in the darkness of early morning. The patrol was drinking hot coffee, eating hot bacon and bisquits. McClellan figured if they were gonna die, it might as well as be on a full stomach. Besides, it was no secret where they were so the fire was okay.

"What's gonna happen today, Dan?"

"Well, Captain, they will make a run at us soon as they can see well enough."He looked up at the graying sky. "It won't be long so we had better muster the men and get them ready."

"They coming from the floor on horses?"

"Could be, but I don't think so. I think they will come on foot moving from rock to rock on the side of the canyon floor. They will come from both the front and the rear and have some on the canyon sides shooting at anyone that lifts their head."
~~~

"MEN,"he shouted. "Gather around me and Dan." When the men were around them he told them what Dan had said. The men looked at one another and then lowered their eyes to the ground. They knew a lot of them were going to die today, maybe all of them. They kneeled there with a look of hopelessness on their faces and in their hearts. McClellan saw this.

"Look men, I know it sounds bad, but as long as there is hope, and I am talking of Tye, we have to fight with our last breath. All of you know Tye and the things he has done in the past. He will get here. It's up to us not to make his efforts wasted. Since there were no shots, no loud screaming and celebrating by the Apache, you have to figure he got away." The men raised their heads and each nodded his understanding. McClellan continued, "Dan here thinks they will make only one attempt to overrun us. If it fails, they will simply wait till we run out of water and food. I want half of you to face up the canyon and half of you the rear, where we come from. They will probably be moving from rock to rock making them tough targets, so take your time and make your shots count. Sergeant, place your men. If they are coming, it will be shortly." The men took up positions where they were placed. They had their pistols out, lying close and handy. They were ready...ready to fight...ready to not make Tye's efforts meaningless by getting killed. They were soldiers...they were ready.

Chapter Nineteen

There was barely enough light to see when they came. The suddness of the attack was shocking. What was more shocking was how close they had gotten during the night. They came from no more than forty yards away, giving the men only time for one shot with their Sharps. Most missed, but McClellan saw two go down and then it was hell. Screaming loudly, the Apaches were on them. McClellan shot one with his pistol and then he lost the pistol when a war club stuck him on the wrist, breaking it. He thrust up with his saber and caught the Apache that had hit him, in the belly with his blade. The Apache had a shocked look on his face as he stood there for a second before McClellan put his boot in the man's stomach and pushed him backwards into another Apache that was coming, intending to kill McClellan. McClellan picked up his pistol with his left hand and shot the brave in the chest before he could recover from being hit by the dead Apache pushed into him.

Garrison was down on one knee, aiming and firing his navy colt with deadly accuracy. Three Apaches lay a few feet in front of him, all shot in the chest. When his hammer hit an empty chamber, he dropped the pistol and pulled his saber. He slashed down at a charging brave intending to cut his screaming head off but the man's left hand came up with a war club and the sword struck it and was deflected away. The Bowie in the Indian's right hand slashed upwards toward the lieutenant's belly. Garrison's quick reflexes saved him. He stepped back and sucked in his belly. The razor sharp blade could not have missed him by more than a half inch. He immediately struck at the man's face with his left fist, striking the Apache on the chin. The brave staggered for an instant, and Garrison came up with his saber, thrusting it into the man's belly. The brave looked down at the sword in his stomach and then at Garrison with a look of pure hate on his face. Garrison raised his left leg and with his foot in the Apache's groin, pushed him back, off his blade. The man collapsed in a heap, never uttering a sound.

Dan had knocked one down with his Sharps, and was swinging his Bowie, forgetting the pain in his shoulder. He was struck a glancing blow on the side of the head with a club and lost conciousness, crumbling to the ground. Another Apache was on him and started his downward thrust with his Bowie when Corporal Langley shot him square thru the brisket. The Apache collapsed on top of Dan. Corporal Langley turned to find another target and was struck in the forehead with a tomahawk, splitting his head open like a ripe watermelon.

Corporal Phipps and Private Christian were standing back to back, swinging their sharps like war clubs. Two Apaches down with busted heads lay by Phipps and one at the feet of Christian. Phipps went down suddenly with an arrow in the shoulder. An Apache that was fixing to attack Phipps before the arrow hit him, jumped over the falling Phipps and was on Christian's back. His left arm was around Christian's throat, and with his Bowie in his right hand, he intended to bury it in the soldiers chest. In a reflex action, Christian throwed his head back, smashing the back of his head into the Apache's face. The warrior was momentarily stunned. In that split second, Christian reached behind him and grabbed a handful of Apache hair. He pulled with all his strength and dropping his right shoulder throwed the Apache over his shoulder and smashing his back hard on the rocky ground. Before the brave could regain his senses, Christian's boot caught the side of his head in a vicious kick, snapping his head sideways and breaking his neck. Then it was over, the

Apache disappearing as fast as they had appeared. For no apparent reason they left when they were close to wiping out the patrol to the last man.

"What the hell?" One trooper hollered. "They had us."

"Dunno," Christian answered. "In one of Tye's talks I remember him saying one could never figure out the mind of an Apache."

The troopers, left standing, were in shock. The viciousness of the attack shook even the most experienced of the troopers. McClellan stood, holding his right wrist against his chest with his left hand.

"Get the dead Apache and put them in a pile over there," he nodded to an area away from where they were. "Get our dead and wounded over there;" pointing behind the rocks with his good hand. "Get the sergeant to get me a casualty report."

"Sergeant's dead sir," a trooper replied.

"Get Corporal Phipps."

"He's down with an arrow in the shoulder, Sir," the private replied.

"Damn," McClellan muttered under his breath. "You private, get me a casualty report and find Garrison."

"Yes Sir."

"I'm here sir," Garrison said coming up behind McClellan. The captain turned toward him and put his good left hand on the lieutenant's shoulder.

"Glad your okay, Lieutenant. Would you get me the status on the water supply and ammunition?"

"Right away, Sir."

McClellan pulled the dead Apache off Dan with his good hand and was relieved his scout was still breathing, though unconscious. His head wound looked superficial but he was going to have a severe headache to go with his shoulder. He suddenly realized his wrist was hurting something awful. The adrenalin that goes through a man in a fight like this sometimes make them forget things like pain and being exhausted until it wears off.

McClellan turned to a private beside him. "Clean Dan's wound and bind up his head."

"Yes Sir. What about your arm, Sir?"

"It'll wait until my men are taken care of." He walked among the huge boulders, looking at his men. Some were dead, others wounded, some would be dead soon from their wounds.

The private he had ordered to get a casualty report came up to him."I have the report sir."

"Go ahead," McClellan ordered.

"Three dead, five wounded seriously and two of them may not make it. Every man has at least a small wound of some kind. Nine Apaches are dead sir; don't know about how many were wounded."

"Very well, private. Good job." He turned to the men and spoke loud enough for all to hear. "I'm proud of each one of you. That was an outstanding job against large odds. Good job," he repeated again. "Now we can lick our wounds and fight again if we have to. According to Dan," he nodded to the uncouncious man, "they won't attack again. They will just try and wait us out. Stay down behind the rocks." Lieutenant Garrison slid in beside him. He had four canteens.

"We poured what water we had into these four canteens. That's all there is. As far as ammunition is concerned, I divided it up and each man that can fight has ten bullets for his Sharps and twenty rounds for his pistol. The wounded each have a pistol with a full cylinder…just in case."

"Thank you Lieutenant. Let the men have a swallow each. You are responsible for the water so make it last."

"Yes Sir."

~~~
~~~

Tye reached the Old Mail Road just as a wagon was coming down the road, headed toward Brackett. He hailed the man driving the wagon. The man, recognizing Tye, hollered.

"My God, Tye. What are you doing out here and where is your horse?" When Tye got close he asked. "Tye, what happened? You look like hell."

"It's a long story friend. Get me to the fort as fast as you can," he said before collapsing in the back of the wagon. The man whipped his horses into a run and the final three miles or so was covered in a short time. He pulled the wagon up to the bridge over Los Moras and hollered at the guard to get some help that he had Tye in the back of the wagon. One of the guards on duty headed toward the post headquarters and Thurston. In about five minutes, Thurston and the post surgeon arrived. They pushed their way through the crowd that had gathered.

The doctor looked Tye over; saw no wounds so he poured water on his face, waking him up. Tye looked around as if trying to figure out where he was. He saw Thurston. "Get a patrol together sir; we have to get back to the patrol before it's too late."

Thurston turned to the private who had summoned him. "Private, you go find Sergeant O'Malley and tell him to put a twenty man patrol together now. Then you go the quartermaster and tell him to get the supplies for twenty men and horses and I want them within an hour."

Tye got off the back of the wagon and stood up. His legs felt like jelly and a man standing next to him held him up.

"What happened, Tye?" Thurston asked. "And where's Sandy?"

Tye quickly told the story, including his running the twenty-five or so miles to get here. Men looked at one another and shook their heads. It was hard to believe a white man could do that, but one just did.

"Get me a horse, Major." Tye said.

"What for? You are going to the hospital."

"Nope; I'm going to be there when we rescue the patrol. I got them into that mess and I'm gonna be there when they get out of it." Thurston took the cigar out of his mouth and started to say something but decided against it. He knew arguing with Tye was a losing battle. "Very well, if you insist," he said cramming the cigar back into his mouth.

Rebbecca and Buff arrived. She threw her arms around Tye's neck and kissed him. She took a step backwards and looked him over. "You're not hurt?"

"Just my feet from running all night."

"I love you, Tye Watkins," she said. "I missed you something terrible."

"I love you to honey," Tye said kissing her on the forehead.

"Yu luke plum tukered out, Tye. Yu sur ya want ta go bac."

"Your right, I'm damn tired, Buff. I got those men into that mess and I'm gonna get them out, if it's the last thing I do."

"I understand yur wanting ta do tha but with yur being this tukered out, are yu gonna be able ta hep."

"The sooner I get this done the quicker I can get back to this," he said taking Rebecca around the waist and pulling her to him. "She just proved how much she loves me."

"And just how did I do that Mr. So Sure of yourself?" Rebecca quizzed.

"By hugging me, kissing me, and not saying anything about the way I smell," he said laughing.

"Now that you mention it," she said and backed off laughing.

"Yu tu shore hav sum strang ways," Buff said laughing with them. Tye walked with them down the bank to Los Moras creek. He layed down and stuck his head under the cold water, then raising it, drank his fill of the best tasting water he had ever had. He lay back on the grass and Rebecca, sitting beside him, raised his head and moved slighty so his head could rest in her lap. She looked at the man she loved and gently wiped the water off his face.

"How many, honey?" she asked.

"How many what?"

"You know, how many were killed.?"

"In my patrol, all but Arnold, Roberts, Christian, and Lieutenant Garrison. At least I think Arnold and Roberts are okay. In the relief patrol that McClellan led, I'm not sure of how many, but it's several."

O'Malley arrived with the patrol and an extra horse.

"Damn, O'Malley that was quick. Couldn't have been more than fifteen minutes since Thurston left," Tye said getting up.

O'Malley laughed. "Hell, I never seen so many men volunteering for a patrol. We just had to wait a few minutes for the supplies."

"Did sawbones assign a man with some medical supplies?"

"Been down this road before, Tye; everything is taken care of." Tye smiled and slapped the shoulder of his father-in-law. "Figured you did."

Tye turned to Rebecca, "I'll be back before dark tomorrow." He gave her a quick kiss drawing some hootin and whistling from the men. There wasn't one of them that didn't wish Rebecca was theirs. They were careful about showing that though because to the man, they had rather face a band of Apaches than face the wrath of Tye. He was easy going most of the time but they had seen or heard of his other side. Tye mounted his horse and the patrol crossed the bridge and headed west at a gallop. Tye would take a less direct route back because the way he had come would be too hard on the horses. It wasn't mid-morning yet and he was certain they would be back at the ambush site before dark.

~~~

McClellan's wrist was paining him something fierce. Garrison had wrapped it the best he could and tied it across his chest. It had swelled to twice its normal size and was dark blue, almost black from below his elbow to his fingertips. Dan was in the same shape with his head and shoulder, they were hurting him too. The prisoner, Cates was one of the few that wasn't hurt in the fight but he had his own pains from the wounds he received when his brother was killed and he was captured. Two of the wounded men were probably going to die if they didn't get medical help soon.

They were in a bad position now. The wounded men were taking a lot of the water. If they weren't careful, they would be out before dark. If Tye didn't make it they were pretty much done for. A few might make it if they made a break for it, but the wounded sure wouldn't. That would be a last resort. They had hurt the Apache pretty good this morning but he had no idea how many were left.He was down to about seven men that could fight and none that were one hundred percent. Their only hope was Tye.

"Do you think he made it to the fort, Sir?" a private asked.

"You can count on it, Private. The devil himself could not stop that man from doing what he sets his mind on doing. He'll be here...count on it."

"Th...tha...thank you,Sir. I... I mean we, looking around at the men, needed to hear that from your lips. If I may say so, Sir, regardless how this turns out, we would like you to know it has been a pleasure riding with you." Each man nodded. Mcclellan could have been knocked over with a feather. He had strived his whole career to be respected and loved by his men. Tye was right, just lead your men and make sound decisions, and stay positive. The men will see that.
~~~

"Thank you men; that means more than you know. Tye will be here, you just wait and see." He turned his back to the men as his eyes teared up. He cleared his throat and turned back to face his men. 'Been a long time coming ole boy; a long time,' he thought.

"Like I said before, men; it's up to us not to make Tye's efforts useless. Take your positions and be ready for anything."

It was mid-morning and it was going to be a typical early fall day, no rain and fairly warm. 'I'm sure glad this isn't summer he thought to himself. We'd already be out of water by now.'

"How you doing, Captain?" McClellan turned around to see Garrison and Dan crouched beside him.

"What about Cates, Sir?" Dan asked.

"What about him?"

"The men want to know about giving him water."

"He's a prisoner and will be treated accordingly," McClellan said... then added "But the sonofabitch gets no water." The men laughed at the out of character cursing by McClellan. Dan thought to himself that McClellan was becoming a first class officer and was human after all. He laughed to himself and thought that Tye would get a laugh out of this. McClellan never cursed and this was twice in two days. Yep, he might just make a good officer

~~~

Tye and the patrol were taking a break, giving the horses a blow. They had covered about half the distance to where McClellan and the patrol were. A new lieutenant by the name of McCallister was in command. He was not a youngster but had come from San Antonio where he had been for over a year. He had been in the service for eight years but had no experience fighting Apaches or anyone else for that matter. He seemed a capable officer to Tye, but Tye had
~~~

overheard Thurston telling the lieutenant to listen to him about any situations where a fight may occur.

They had stopped at Val Verde Springs. The spring was always running but not as much volume of water as was produced by Los Moras Springs at Clark. The water was cold and there was plenty of shade under the oaks and pecan trees that surrounded the spring. It was a pleasant place to rest but the situation didn't allow the men to enjoy it. They all knew of the importance of making it to the patrol before dark and when the order was given to mount up, there was none of the usual grumbling from them.

Tye, instead of being out front, was riding beside McCallister. This was the first time McCallister had been out here so Tye felt he needed to spend time pointing out certain things about the area such as springs, trails, and dead end canyons. The dead end canyons, canyons with only one way in and one way out, could be fatal if one led men into it. Tye liked the lieutenant. He reminded him of another Lieutenant that had become a damn good officer, Lieutenant Garrison. He had become a good friend of Tye's also.

The miles were passing quickly under the horses hooves. Even the horses seemed to sense the urgency of their mission. The land was fairly flat now and would be till they got within four or five miles of their destination. It was all cactus, cedar, and purple sage that covered the landscape. After the rain yesterday, it was pretty, the green of the cedars and light purple or pink of the sage against the almost white land. The patrol, with the horses steel shoes striking rocks and the rattling of the sabers, reminded Tye again why the army could never seem to surprise the Apache.

After another break in the afternoon, Tye halted the patrol. There was about two hours of daylight left.

"Lieutenant, we are about a half mile of where McClellan is. I suggest you and the men stay here and let me scout things out; shouldn't be gone more than thirty minutes or so."

McCallister turned to his sergeant and told him to have the men dismount and take a break. He dismounted, handed the reins of his horse to a private and walked to a little knoll to watch for Tye.

Tye, lying on his belly behind some sage looked through the binoculars. He could see where the soldiers were but could not see them. As he watched, he saw the Apaches mounting their ponies. "Sonofabitch," he said. "They are fixing to try and overrun the patrol." He was surprised at the number of Apaches. 'There must have been more ride in,' he thought to himself. He was looking at close to thirty warriors. He slid back down the hill and mounted his horse and was at a dead run to get back to McCallister. Every second was important now.

McCallister saw him coming and had the patrol mounted when Tye arrived.

Tye quickly explained the situation and they might just get lucky and trap the Apaches in the canyon. The Indians would be trapped by their own doing by blocking the other end with the boulders. Within minutes the patrol was in a skirmish line close to the canyon but behind a hill. Tye dismounted and scrambled up the hill. Just as he looked over he saw the Apache starting their attack. Within seconds, Tye was back down and mounted. It was time to turn the table on the Apache; at least he hoped they would.

Chapter Twenty

McClellan and the men saw the Apaches gathered at the entrance, maybe a quarter mile away. He had all his men, all seven, facing them. He looked up at the sun which was close to dropping behind the canyon rim. Where was Tye?

He looked at his men and saw the desperation in their faces. Some were mumbling to themselves, probabling praying. They all knew what was coming and it would be over in a few minutes.

With screams splitting the air, they came. The soldiers braced themselves as they intended to take as many of the Apaches down as they could before they were over whelmed.

"HOLD," McClellan shouted. "HOLD," he repeated. At fifty yards he gave the order, "FIRE," and seven rifles fired and seven riderless ponies were breaking away from the rest. "FIRE AT WILL," McClelland screamed and the men were blasting away with their pistols as arrows and bullets slammed into where they were. McClellan went down with an arrow in the shoulder and Dan a bullet in the leg. Another man took an arrow in the chest and died. At Twenty yards the Apache swerved away much to the surprise of the doomed troopers. A second later they heard it too, a bugle blowing charge. Looking past the Apache, they saw the patrol charging down the canyon. The Apaches, realizing they were trapped knew the only way out was through the charging troopers. Twenty or so Apaches charged the troopers. At one hundred yards the order was given to dismount and lay the horses down. The men, lying behind their horses took aim. At forty yards

McCallister gave the order to fire. Bullets from the troopers met bullets and arrows from the Apaches in a deadly rain of death. The Apaches were expert marksman from a running horse and their aim was deadly, but so were the troopers. Only six warriors jumped their horses over the troopers causing the soldiers to grab some dirt to escape the ponies' hooves. As the Apaches rode away, another three were knocked off their ponies and one was slumped over his pony's neck. McCallister stood up and looked left and right at his troopers. He could see four that appeared dead and two more wounded.

Tye was already on his horse and headed toward McClellan and the men he had left yesterday. The men were yelling and waving their arms. Tears of happiness streamed down their faces as they come from behind the rocks and made their way to Tye, There was a lot of back slapping and hugging but Tye was looking for McClellan. He saw Garrison and waved at him.

"Where's the Captain and Dan?" his question asked to no one in particular.

"They are still behind the rocks, Tye. They both are hit," one trooper said. Tye ran over to where they were and was grateful to see both of them smiling.

"Took your damn time didn't you?" McClellan said smiling.

"You know me, Captain, I always like the dramatic entrance," Tye said laughing and walked over to Dan and shook his hand. The rest of the patrol arrived and there was a lot of laughing and hugging not necessarily between soldiers but between friends. For a lot of soldiers, the only family they had was their fellow soldiers.

"See the damn 'patches didn't kill you, you stinking sonofabitch," Yancy screamed. It got real quite all of a sudden as the soldiers watched. Tye walked over to him and seen his cracked and swollen lips.

"Thirsty, Yancey?" he asked as he took the canteen he had and took a big swallow. The other men had gotten water from the patrol. Tye took the canteen and held it in front of him about six inches from Yancy's face. "Like a drink, Yancy?" He poured the water on the ground and walked off leaving Yancy screaming and cursing and calling Tye and the army all sorts of vile names.

"You can cuss all you want, Yancy. It won't help you none. You have a date with the hangman at Brackett," Tye said smiling and walking away.

"I ain't back to the fort yet you bastard. I ain't gonna hang and when I get away it will the sorriest day of your stinking life. I hear your wife's real purty," Yancy yelled. Tye stopped in mid stride, turned and walked back to Yancy. All talk among the men stopped because they knew this outlaw just made a big mistake. Tye slapped him hard across the face.

"WHAT ARE YOU DOING, TYE?" screamed McClellan.

"Nothing. Just going to tell this piece of shit what I'm thinking." None of the men felt sorry for Yancy, in fact they all knew he made a mistake when he mentioned Rebecca. They also were sure they didn't want to ever say anything out of line about Rebecca that might get back to Tye. The look on his face was enough to make a man cringe.

"I'm gonna tell you something, Yancey," Tye said. "I hope you do escape because when you do, I'm coming after you...by myself. There will be no soldiers or soldier rules to protect you. I promise you the slowest, most painful death a man can think of. There is nothing an Apache can do to a man that I can't do better. That's my promise to you." Yancey sat down, startled at Tye's threat. He said nothing else.

The wounded was on travois' and the dead were tied to their horses. The men were in good spirts as they headed back to the fort, and home. The trooper leading the horse the wounded Yancy was on had to listen to his tirads aimed at the army and Tye. Sometimes his ranting was loud enough for all to hear. "TYE WATKINS YOU BASTARD. I SWEAR I'M GONNA KILL YOU CAUSE I AIN'T GONNA HANG. YOUR STINKING SOLDIER BOYS WILL NEVER HOLD OLD YANCY."

The trooper leading Yancy's horse turned and backhanded him shutting him up. About twenty soldiers, counting the wounded and the officers smiled at the trooper. Tye was thinking that he would be glad when this patrol was over and Yancy was behind bars. He had brought in a lot of men over the years…some real bad ones but he thought Yancy was the worse of the lot. Yancy was just bad through and through and hated the Yankee army with a passion. Hell, he just hated everybody. He and his brother had killed no telling how many innocent men and raped a lot of wives and young girls. 'This country will be a lot better off when he is dead.'

"Tye, the trooper with Yancy says that the sonofabitch wants to see you," a corporal riding behind Tye said. Tye turned Sandy and headed back to where Yancy was. McClellan and McCallister were hot on his heels to make sure he didn't kill this piece of horse dung.

"What do you want, Yancy?" Tye asked sharply.

"Just wanted to say that you beat the hell out of me; I had my chance but you did it anyway."

"Just get to the damn point, Yancy."

"Just saying that you should have killed me because you ain't gonna get another chance. When I get out of your damn guardhouse, I'll kill you first time I lay eyes on you."

"You're not getting out, Yancy. You are going to hang and for the first time I am going to watch a man I brought in die on the gallows. I think I will enjoy it too."

"We ain't there yet…not by a long shot," Yancy yelled at Tye who was riding back up to the front of the patrol. He pushed his hate of Yancy aside and thought of something better…a reunion with his wife. “Oh yeah,’ he thought to himself smiling. ‘More stories from Shakespear too.”

www.ingramcontent.com/pod-product-compliance
Lightning Source LLC
Chambersburg PA
CBHW030446250626
47154CB00003BA/1148

* 9 7 8 0 9 7 9 4 4 4 3 9 5 *